"Where Are You?" She Screamed. "Tell Me Where You Are So I Can Help You!"

She was sobbing now, because the call had been so desperate, so pleading, and she recognized the pain, the loneliness, as deep and as real as her own—

"—youuu—"

Me, she thought wildly. *It's me he wants; he wants me, he needs me, I've got to help him somehow—*

"Please! *Where are you?*"

She was as far as she could go now, standing on the balcony, her hands curled around the railing, and she could feel the soggy weight of her nightgown whipping around her, and her hair streaming wildly in the wind, and she leaned forward, straining far, far over the endless abyss of the night—

She didn't hear the boards giving out beneath her.

Didn't hear the sudden groan and snap of old wood, the rusty creak of the railing swinging away . . .

Books by Richie Tankersley Cusick

BUFFY, THE VAMPIRE SLAYER
(a novelization based on the screenplay by Joss Whedon)
THE DRIFTER
FATAL SECRETS
HELP WANTED
THE LOCKER
THE MALL
SILENT STALKER
VAMPIRE

Available from ARCHWAY Paperbacks

RICHIE TANKERSLEY
CUSICK

The Drifter

YA
CUS

AN ARCHWAY PAPERBACK
Published by POCKET BOOKS
New York   London   Toronto   Sydney   Tokyo   Singapore

This book is a work of fiction. Names, characters, places and incidents are products of the author's imagination or are used fictitiously. Any resemblance to actual events or locales or persons, living or dead, is entirely coincidental.

AN ARCHWAY PAPERBACK *Original*

An Archway Paperback published by
POCKET BOOKS, a division of Simon & Schuster Inc.
1230 Avenue of the Americas, New York, NY 10020

ISBN: 0-671-88741-6

First Archway Paperback printing July 1994

10 9 8 7 6 5 4 3 2 1

AN ARCHWAY PAPERBACK and colophon are registered trademarks of Simon & Schuster Inc.

Cover art by Gerber Studio

Printed in the U.S.A.

IL 6+

For Wayne . . .
Happy Birthday
Happy Always

1

"SOME SAY YOU CAN STILL HEAR THEM — VOICES OF POOR, drowned sailors. Even now."

The tall, gaunt housekeeper looked down at Carolyn Baxter and her mother, who were huddled together at the bottom of the front steps. Wind moaned around the eaves of the house, and a light fog was already swirling along the ground at their feet.

"What you mean is," Mrs. Baxter said firmly, "the ocean only *sounds* like voices calling. Isn't that it?"

Nora's lips stretched into a macabre semblance of a smile.

"On deep, dark nights," she monotoned, "calling out their own names . . . as drowned men's ghosts are said to do."

Carolyn shivered, casting an anxious glance at the clouds scudding across the pewter-gray sky. She could hear the ocean, and she knew it was very close, but the fog was closing in so fast now, obscuring everything from view, even most of the house that loomed up before them.

"If I'd known you were coming tonight, I'd have said wait till morning." Nora raked them with a chilly frown. "But I *didn't* know. No one told *me.*"

"How . . . how did they drown?" Carolyn asked, not even aware that she'd stepped closer to her mother. She nervously fingered the tiny gold chain she always wore around her neck, and slipped it down inside her collar.

"Many a ship's been lured to those cliffs, to crash on the rocks below." Nora raised one thin eyebrow and tilted her head slightly, as if studying the girl. "Watery graves, the lot of them."

"Sounds like legend and superstition to me," Mrs. Baxter countered lightly.

Nora gazed at them and said nothing.

"It isn't supposed to be cold like this in summer." Carolyn gave a nervous laugh, eager to change the subject. "Nobody told me I should have brought winter clothes to the beach."

Nodding, her mother put a hand on Carolyn's arm. "This horrible fog," Mrs. Baxter mumbled, casting a glance behind her, into oblivion. "I can hardly see a thing. I'd be afraid to take a single step away from the house until it cleared."

"You're wise to be cautious." Nora spoke crisply as she shoved a key into the front door. "Some haven't been. And they've gone to their deaths over those cliffs."

"Really?" Carolyn shivered. "How close are they?"

"Not fifty feet from where you stand." Nora made a

vague gesture. "The house sits practically on the edge. Didn't you know?"

Mrs. Baxter sounded apologetic. "Not really. We only learned about Aunt Hazel's death a week ago. We hadn't been in touch with her for such a long time . . ."

"Hmmph," Nora sniffed, giving the door a shove. "I believe *that!* I worked for her this whole past year, and she never said a word about *you!*" She glanced back, narrowing her flinty eyes. "Nobody said you'd be here tonight. Folks around here were real *surprised* she left Glanton House to you. She loved this place. She was *particular* about who stayed."

Carolyn looked down at her shoes, fascinated by the little swirls of fog snaking around her ankles. It was obvious that Nora didn't approve of them *or* of them being here. Why couldn't Mom take the hint and just turn right around and head back for Ohio?

"It was a godsend for us, really." Mom was trying to be pleasant, going ahead of Carolyn up the steps and onto the sagging porch. "Hazel is—*was*—my great-aunt on my father's side, but I didn't really know her. The family was never what you'd call close."

Why is she telling this weird woman about us? Carolyn wondered. She saw the way Nora's piercing eyes bore into them, her lips set in a tight line, and it made Carolyn's skin crawl. *She hates us, can't Mom see that, so why don't we just quit talking and leave?*

"My husband died recently . . ." There was a catch in Mom's voice, but she swallowed it and hurried on. "I've always wanted to run a guest house, and Carolyn and I desperately needed the income. So of course, when I found out Aunt Hazel had left us this place, I wanted to see it as soon as possible, and that's why—"

"Won't get many guests out this way." Nora's face settled into a sneer. "Too far out from the mainland. Not enough sun. Too windy."

Carolyn realized she was nodding in silent agreement. The whole time they'd been standing there, she'd been uneasily conscious of the sharp wind, howling and shrieking around the house, biting through her summer clothes until her skin felt raw.

"But surely Aunt Hazel had visitors from time to time," Mom was going on as Nora turned back to the door. It seemed to be stuck, and the woman leaned her weight against it.

"No. She liked her solitude. She didn't have much use for people."

"So why's it called Glanton House?" Carolyn asked. "Aunt Hazel's name was Crawford."

"Named after the sea captain who built it," Nora said shortly. She rammed her shoulder, and the door popped open, banging back into darkness. "It's true, what I said. About the poor dead sailors. Him, too. You'll see."

"Him? You mean Captain—" Carolyn began, but Nora slipped into the house, motioning Mrs. Baxter to follow.

Carolyn watched the two women disappear into the shadows. Then she stepped back and looked slowly over the house, from the porch all the way to the roof.

It was gray . . . as gray and nondescript as the fog hanging heavy around it, its outside walls weathered by long seasons of salt spray and raw wind and damp

4

piercing cold. It rose, shuttered and shingled, with bays and gables, spires and cupolas, wrapped all around with a porch, and oddly distorted in the soupy mist. As Carolyn's gaze swept over the chimneys and rooftops, she drew her breath in slowly.

A widow's walk.

Right up there, at the very top of the house.

A railed platform encircling a small wooden garret —the attic, she guessed—*where some woman . . . at some time . . . must have kept watch out to sea for the return of someone she loved. . . .*

The captain Nora had mentioned? Carolyn loved legends. She'd have to ask Nora to finish that story about Captain Glanton.

She stared at the widow's walk another few minutes, then lowered her brown eyes to the porch, giving a long, deep shiver. She was damp and chilled straight through to her bones. Gathering her dark hair back from her face, she turned to look sideways past the house.

No . . . she couldn't really see the water beyond the veil of fog, but she could hear it—she could smell it—every sense tingled with the uneasy awareness that it was *there,* just beyond the grayness, water and water and more water, and that strange feeling that it was watching . . . that it was waiting . . .

Carolyn shuddered again and ran up the steps, making her way into a dingy parlor as the other two women continued an argument.

"Well, anyway," Mrs. Baxter said briskly. "That's our plan."

"Stupid plan, if you ask me," Nora replied.

"Well, I'm not asking you." Mrs. Baxter frowned, and Nora regarded her with a look of half surprise, half indignation.

"So you've worked here for the last year," Mom went on firmly, and the flinty-gray eyes narrowed as Nora waited for her to finish.

"She couldn't have done without me," Nora said.

"And I'm sure it'd be difficult for *me* to do without you, too," Mom added. "So I'd like you to stay, if you think you can stand to be a little more pleasant."

Nora's back was ramrod straight. Her spidery hands plucked at the plain black dress she was wearing, then slid up to pat the bun into place at the back of her neck.

"I'll think about it," Nora said.

"You do that," Mom answered, and Carolyn saw her turn away to hide a smile. "Goodness, it's so cold in here. So damp."

"Been empty, that's why. Didn't expect you tonight, like I said. Been locked up."

"Can't we turn the heat on or something?" Mom sighed. *"Is* there heat?"

"Of course there's heat," Nora sniffed, giving Mom a look that implied she was a total idiot. "But it'll take a while for it to start working."

"Fine. Just turn it on." Mrs. Baxter waited till Nora left the room, then turned to Carolyn with a groan. "Look at this mess. Oh, Carolyn, what have we done? What have I gotten us into?"

It *was* pretty bad, Carolyn had to admit, taking a long, slow survey of the room. The parlor furniture was draped in dingy yellowed sheets. The wallpaper was peeling and stained with mildew. Damp gray ashes had blown from the fireplace, scattering across the area rug and the wooden floor, and a heavy dank odor hung in the air with the tangy smell of the sea. Beyond the windowpanes fog curled silently, as if eavesdropping on their conversation.

Nora reappeared in the doorway, shrugging out of her sweater. Her sleeves were long and black, tapered to her wrists. She reminded Carolyn of a skeleton in mourning.

"Better come along," Nora muttered, "if you want to see the rest of it."

Carolyn and her mother exchanged looks and obediently followed Nora on a tour of the house. There were two bedrooms on the first floor, a bathroom, a dining room with a huge oval table, and a kitchen at the very back, large and old-fashioned and sadly outdated. Mom eyed the rust-spotted sink and tiny refrigerator, and Carolyn heard her moan again.

"This way," Nora said, and they turned and followed her up a wide wooden staircase to the second floor. "More bedrooms up here."

As she led them from doorway to doorway, Carolyn stared in amazement. The rooms were a good size, their dark, massive furniture shrouded in dropcloths and dust, and yellowed shades hung at the windows, casting a jaundiced glow through the rooms. All Carolyn could think of was a funeral home.

"Candles by the beds," Nora informed them. "Wind's always knocking the electric out. There're flashlights, too, but the batteries probably don't work." She jabbed a finger toward one end of the hall.

"Another bathroom there. Plumbing's not great. Takes forever for water to get hot. Best be warned about that."

"Oh, look Carolyn," Mom said, her voice lifting. "A claw-footed tub! You know, with the right curtains and wallpaper, this bathroom could be really charming! Potpourri and candles and fresh, fluffy guest towels—"

But Carolyn scarcely heard her. She was still standing in the first bedroom Nora had shown them, studying it uncertainly. It was nothing at all like her sunny room at home, but maybe . . . *with a lot of work* . . .

She walked slowly from wall to wall, lifting the edges of the dropcloths. There was a white iron bedstead and a vanity table, a wicker rocking chair, and an embroidered footstool. On one wall hung a grimy mirror, and as she walked closer, her own reflection stared back at her, oddly distorted. Startled, she gave a cry, then laughed at herself. *Silly, what did you think it was . . . ghosts?*

Windows faced her on two sides, with the insistent pounding of the sea beyond, but Carolyn resisted the urge to raise the shades and look out. Instead she opened the doors of an armoire, but found it disappointingly empty. Walking back out into the hallway, she found Nora and her mother still talking in the bathroom, and as she waited for them to finish, she noticed a narrow door at the very rear of the corridor.

Intrigued, Carolyn went over and tried the latch, but it wouldn't turn. Gripping harder, she twisted again, but the thing refused to budge.

"It's locked," said a voice behind her, and Carolyn

8

nearly jumped out of her skin. Whirling around, she saw Nora's face hovering over her shoulder, the woman's eyes gleaming in the half light.

"Oh, Nora, you scared me!" Carolyn gasped. "I didn't hear you—"

"Always locked," Nora said stiffly. "She wanted it that way."

"Hazel?" Carolyn asked. "Then where does it go?" She fell back a step as Nora advanced.

"Above. To the widow's walk."

A shiver went through Carolyn. She glanced again at the door.

"Can I see it?"

"Too dangerous. Hasn't been used for years and years. And anyway, I don't have the key."

"Well, where is it?"

"I'm sure I don't know." Nora turned abruptly and headed for the stairs, though her voice floated back to where Carolyn was standing. "Best leave it as it is. Don't want accidents, do you?"

"We don't have to *leave* it unlocked," Carolyn said, following slowly behind. She could hear her mother back down below, yanking sheets off furniture, shaking them, coughing. "I just want to see what it looks like, that's all."

Nora stopped and turned back toward her. Her face was like a pale, pinched mask, dark eyes glittering with a strange light.

"It's an evil place," Nora said softly. "And now I've warned you."

2

"SO WHAT CAN YOU TELL US?" MRS. BAXTER ASKED curiously. "About the house, I mean?"

They were sitting at the kitchen table, and Nora was at the stove, her back to them, fussing with a teakettle. For a long moment she didn't answer, then finally her shoulders seemed to square a little, and she turned on the burner with a deft flick of her wrist.

"Captain Glanton built it," she said. "Many years ago—back in the eighteen hundreds. It was for his bride. They were very young and very much in love, if the story's to be believed."

Carolyn settled down in her chair and propped her arms on the tabletop, resting her chin in her hands. Beside her, Mrs. Baxter gave a wink and again urged Nora to continue.

"But he was a captain, like I said," Nora went on solemnly, "and everyone knows that a captain's first love—*only* true love, really—is the sea. *She* couldn't keep him here, that young wife of his. She never could keep him here for long."

"And so he built the widow's walk for her," Carolyn interjected. "So she could watch for him to come home from his journeys?"

Mrs. Baxter ruffled her daughter's hair affectionately. "You'll have to forgive Carolyn, Nora. My daughter's a hopeless romantic."

Nora shot a quick, dark glance over her shoulder. It settled on Carolyn, then flicked away again.

"He did build the walk for her," Nora spoke slowly, as if carefully choosing her words. "And he did swear to return, and she promised she'd wait. But she was a young thing, as I said—young and pretty and foolish. And the days turned into weeks, and the weeks into months. Then one day she grew tired of waiting and decided he must have met with a tragic fate. And so she loved another."

"Even though her husband might still have been alive?" Carolyn fretted, and Mrs. Baxter shook her head in amusement.

"A drifter, he was, looking for work. And she needed the help of a man around, and so she let him stay on."

"And they fell in love?" Carolyn guessed.

"Her new happiness was not to be," Nora said stiffly. "The lover was a cruel man, as she soon found out—jealous and spiteful—and she grew more and more unhappy. And then one night the storm came."

Nora paused. Carolyn leaned forward in her chair and gripped the edge of the table.

"Go on, Nora—please—"

"The fiercest storm of the decade, with winds and floods and many lives lost. That was the night Captain Glanton's ship came home at last. *She* saw it coming —standing up there on the widow's walk—*she* saw it coming toward land . . . and she watched as it was dashed to pieces on the rocks below."

Carolyn felt as if she'd been hit in the stomach. She lowered her hands from her face and stared incredulously.

"You mean . . . she saw it *happen?* Right in front of her? Her husband killed on the very night he finally came home?"

"Carolyn"—Mom shook her head—"honey, it's only a story."

"Men and women alike braved the storm that night, looking for survivors up and down the coast. And it's said that her lover did indeed find Captain Glanton— barely alive and reaching out his hand for help."

"So the lover saved him?" Carolyn asked breathlessly.

Nora's dark eyes flashed. "It was a knife he took . . . and *chopped* off the captain's hand. And then he stood watching . . . and smiling . . . as the captain sank helplessly back into the sea."

"Oh, my God . . ." Carolyn whispered.

"They never found the captain's body," Nora murmured. "Though they searched for many a day."

"What about the crew?" Carolyn asked anxiously.

"None survived. And they lie there still . . . at the bottom of the ocean. Every one."

For an endless moment there was silence. At last Mrs. Baxter leaned forward in her chair and patted Carolyn's arm.

"Carolyn, it's just folklore, honey—"

"What happened to Captain Glanton's wife?" Carolyn asked.

"They say she lost her mind," Nora went on, opening cupboard doors, pulling cups and saucers down, dusting them with her dish towel. "She never spoke again. And every day after . . . and each night, too . . . she kept watch from the walk above, always believing that somehow—still—her husband would come home to her as he'd always promised he would."

"But . . ." Carolyn whispered, "he didn't."

Nora turned around. Her face was cold and impassive, her words brusque.

"They found her not long after. Dead and all alone—her lover gone who knows where. No one ever knew."

"So . . ." Carolyn murmured, "he *killed* her? How?"

"Her throat was ripped clean away."

Carolyn's hand went unconsciously to her own throat. "Where did they find her?"

"Here. In Glanton House."

"But . . . *where* in the house?"

Nora shrugged and shook her head. "She's buried in the village churchyard, even now. But hardly at rest, they say. She keeps watch for him . . and he searches for her to this very day."

Mrs. Baxter groaned, and Nora regarded her coldly.

"Laugh if you will, but Hazel believed it. Lots of folks around here do. That's why I never stay at night. It's a house for the dead . . . not the living."

Once more the silence fell. Once more Mrs. Baxter broke it.

"Well, it's a tragic story . . . a touching story . . . and it'll make *great* publicity for our guesthouse, don't you think so, Carolyn?"

"What was her name?" Carolyn asked, and Nora turned off the stove as the teakettle shrieked.

"Oh, Carolyn, really!" Mrs. Baxter laughed.

"Do you know, Nora?" Carolyn insisted.

For a long moment Nora said nothing. Then her voice sounded again, low and precise. *"His* was Matthew. Captain Matthew Glanton. And hers was . . . Carolyn."

Carolyn's gasp was loud in the uneasy quiet. She glanced fearfully around the kitchen as though the captain himself might walk through the door at any moment.

"Well, there you go!" Mrs. Baxter said brightly. "My goodness, Carolyn, I think it's a sign! We really *were* meant to come here!"

But Carolyn didn't answer. She ran her hands slowly along her arms, trying to rub the goose bumps away. She was only half-conscious of Nora putting a steaming cup of tea down in front of her. She stared hard at Nora's clawlike hands and pale, pointed nails.

"Seriously now," Mrs. Baxter spoke up, "after all these years of that story being handed down, generation to generation, a lot of the original facts have probably been distorted! Suppose the captain didn't miss his wife at all? Suppose while he was off playing on the high seas, he fell in love with someone else? And he really wanted a divorce when he got back?" She frowned, thinking. "Hmmm . . . perhaps some native girl on some exotic island . . ."

"Oh, Mom"—Carolyn sounded exasperated—

14

"you can ruin a beautiful story quicker than anyone I know!"

Her mother feigned innocence. "Well, I'm just being sensible! We don't really know, do we? I mean, there're no eyewitnesses, are there?"

"You're impossible," Carolyn said grudgingly and got up and went into the parlor. She could hear Nora and her mother talking quietly in the background, but she couldn't make out what they were saying— *probably Mom telling her not to fill my head with nonsense.*

Sighing, she walked slowly to the dining room window and peered out into the fog. Even the glass was wet inside, and the room trembled with every gust of wind. She felt clammy all over, as if the sea spray were creeping in through the nooks and crevices of the old house, seeping deep into her soul. . . .

I don't care if it is only a legend . . . it's still the most haunting story I've ever heard.

For just the briefest moment there was a break in the fog, and Carolyn stared out at the shadowy surroundings. No trees . . . not a single neighbor in sight. But Nora had been right about one thing—the coastline *was* close to the house—*too close,* Carolyn thought uneasily. She could see now that the house sat on a ledge jutting out from the mainland and into the water, and as far as she could see there was ocean. It seemed to stretch forever, as gray and miserable as the fog.

Carolyn clutched the windowsill to keep from swooning. *Is this what being seasick is?* Suddenly she felt so lonely . . . so vulnerable . . . so isolated that she fought back tears and closed her eyes.

She stood that way for several minutes, waiting for the dizziness to pass. Then once more she opened her eyes.

A chill crept up her spine.

She drew in her breath and leaned in closer to the window, wiping at the pane with her fingertips.

There was *another* shape out there now . . . something that hadn't been there only a moment ago—vague and blurry—ghostlike through the fog. *A person?*

It was impossible to tell for sure, but somehow she had the impression it might be a man—someone tall—someone just standing there, not moving, staring at the house . . .

Carolyn hurried to the front door and flung it open. She went out onto the porch and strained her eyes through the fog, opening her mouth to call.

But the fog streamed around her, empty.

And the mournful shriek of the wind sounded almost like a human cry for help.

3

CAROLYN COULDN'T SLEEP.

She'd tried hard to be cheerful through dinner, tried to be cordial when Nora had finally gone home, tried even harder to be enthusiastic over Mom's growing list of plans for their guesthouse. But now she was tired of pretending, and so she lay in her unfamiliar bed in her unfamiliar room and tried to shut out the distant roar of the sea. *Only it's not so distant,* she thought gloomily, *it's practically in our front yard.*

She could hear it churning forward at full speed . . . sounding for all the world as if it would crash over the house and swallow it whole. And then, after a moment, receding again . . . softening . . . going quiet and hushed, the calm before the inevitable storm.

At this particular instant it was ebbing, and Carolyn braced herself for the onslaught to come. For the hundredth time she flopped over on her stomach and bunched her pillow around her head.

It was no use.

The ocean was just *there*—instead of birds or traffic or conversation or even silence. Just *there* going on and on forever.

Carolyn groaned and sat up. She scooted back against the headboard and pulled her knees up to her chin, clasping her arms around them. Her heart ached with homesickness, for her friends, for Dad. She'd hoped for a cozy cottage on a sunny beach. Instead she'd gotten Glanton House and Nora.

She sighed. "My luck."

Something thumped against the side of the house, and she stifled a scream. Throwing off the covers, she padded to the window and saw a loose shutter banging in the wind. The fog was so thick, she couldn't even see the ground below.

Carolyn leaned against the sill, staring out into nothingness. It gave her a strange feeling of unreality, this being suspended in a darkly swirling void. She stood there for a long time and tried not to give in to tears. And then at last she turned back to her bed.

Halfway across the floor, she froze.

She caught her breath and held it, and then she waited.

And it wasn't the sea she heard this time—not the sea or even the wind—but something different. Something hushed and hidden and muffled, coming from the floor above.

As Carolyn stood there and listened, it hit the wall with a soft thud, and then it slid. Hit . . . then slid. Hit . . . slid.

No, Carolyn thought wildly as her brain reeled to

identify the sound—*not sliding exactly—but rougher —more uneven—*

Scraping?

Yes, that was it, she decided, more like scraping— no—like *clawing*—like something *clawing* at the wood of the walls—

"She keeps watch for him . . . and he searches for her to this very day. . . ."

Carolyn pressed herself back against the wall, her heart slowly freezing. In her mind she quickly tried to reconstruct the lay of the house, the location of each upstairs room. Was it possible the strange sounds were coming from some other bedroom on this floor? She closed her eyes and drew a deep, slow breath. No . . . the sounds had definitely come from above.

The widow's walk?

She tried to picture it as she'd seen it earlier that evening—the railed platform and the small wooden garret it surrounded—and she remembered thinking it must be a sort of attic, or maybe just an empty storage room—

Except it wasn't empty now.

Carolyn spun around, her eyes groping through darkness. Quickly she found her bedside lamp and turned the switch.

Nothing happened.

She tried it again.

Still nothing.

Trembling now, she felt for the matches on the table and lit the candle beside them. A sickly puddle of yellow light spread out across the floor, sending macabre shadows along the corners and ceiling. She moved noiselessly out into the corridor, and then she stopped. She could see the wooden door at the end of the hallway—could see the latch upon it that had no key.

She held her breath and waited.

A gust of wind shook the house, rattling the windows in their frames. The ancient boards pulled and groaned, and the broken shutter crashed wildly against the outside wall of her room.

It must have been like this that night the captain came home—only much, much worse because of the storm—the whole house heaving and swaying while the ship tore open on the rocks below and spilled her men into the sea—

And at first Carolyn didn't even hear the long, low groaning sound—the stubborn cry of warped wood tearing away from long-stuck hinges.

But as she continued to stare at that narrow door, she suddenly realized it was *moving*—inch by inch— until at last it stood partway open, a pitch-black sliver in the wall.

Her lungs ached, and she realized she'd been holding her breath. She let it out slowly and felt the candle tremble in her outstretched hand.

It's only the wind . . . it's gotten through the cracks and made a terrible draft, and now the door's blown open because it's so old . . . that's all it is. . . .

Yet as she moved cautiously toward it, such a feeling of dread came over her that she had to stop and choke back a cry and then force herself to go on again.

"Only the wind," she whispered to herself, *"only the wind—only the—"*

But the eerie sound came again from somewhere above her, and there was no mistaking it this time— that soft thud against wood, and then the long . . . slow . . . scraping . . .

Carolyn lifted her candle and peered fearfully through the opening. A steep staircase flickered into view and led straight up inside the walls.

"It's much too dangerous . . . I don't have the key." She could hear Nora's voice again, as plain as day. *"It hasn't been used for years. . . ."*

"Then why is it open now?" Carolyn whispered to herself "Why now?"

She didn't want to go up there.

Every instinct warned her against it, screamed at her to slam the door and shove something in front of it, to run away and never get this close to it again.

"Hello?" she called, and her voice echoed back to her hollowly. "Is someone up there? Mom? Is that you?"

No answer.

The silence was almost worse than the sounds.

Carolyn cupped one hand protectively around the candle flame and began to climb.

The stairs smelled of mildew and rot. They creaked and groaned underfoot as if each step she took might shatter them to bits. Carolyn moved slowly . . . carefully . . . eyes darting back and forth as she made her way above. Hidden things scurried around her in the walls; spiderwebs wrapped stickily around her face. She fought down panic, and at last felt the floor level out beneath her feet.

"Hello?" she whispered. "Is anyone up—"

Her voice broke, and she stared. It *was* a room—an

attic, just like she'd thought—full of murky shadows and filmy cobwebs that shimmered like phantoms in the candlelight. There was no furniture, no decoration of any kind, save for a messy heap of boxes and trunks against one far wall. For just a second Carolyn thought she saw movement among the clutter, but as her eyes riveted in on the pile, everything lay silent and still. Nervously she turned toward the door that led out to the widow's walk.

Again she lifted her candle.

The flame fluttered dangerously, and the walls seemed to breathe around her.

I was right—there's nothing up here—it was only the wind after all.

She could see that the door had a wooden bolt, and that the bolt was slid all the way back, leaving the door unbarred.

Carolyn moved toward it, scarcely conscious of the floorboards groaning beneath her feet. She stopped in front of the door and slowly reached out for the knob.

A blast of wind tore through the attic.

It shrieked through every crack and crevice, shivering the floor and vibrating the walls.

As if alive, the doorknob jerked in her hand, pulling the opposite way as she tried to turn it. Carolyn screamed and let go. Panicking, she backed toward the stairs, but the candle flame suddenly flared, illuminating the other walls around her.

Her blood turned to ice. She stared at the walls, and a second scream rose into her throat.

Every wall was scraped and cut, spattered with dark spreading stains. There were deep gouges in the wood as though something had dug in with great force and then pulled out again. As Carolyn stared in disbelief, she could see that the runny splatters had hit the ceiling—sprayed up onto the rafters and dripped down into corners, leaving smeared patterns wherever they touched.

Carolyn felt sick. Transfixed by the grisly scene, she was suddenly aware of a movement from the corner of her eye, and as she slowly faced the widow's walk, her eyes widened in terror.

Someone was in the doorway.

Trapped within the swirling fog, the figure hovered there—*floated* there—clothes and hair billowing darkly in the wind . . .

"No," Carolyn choked, "no . . ."

Ghostly arms lifted into the air . . . ghostly hands fluttered weakly at a throat Carolyn couldn't see . . .

But she *could* see the thick, wet pool upon the floor as it oozed slowly toward her and puddled around her bare feet.

Carolyn bolted for the stairs.

She tried to call for help, but without warning the floor disappeared, and she pitched down . . . down . . . into blackness.

4

"We can do this," Mrs. Baxter said firmly, looking up as Carolyn appeared in the kitchen doorway. "We can do this, I know we can. We can make this work and—" She sat straighter and peered at Carolyn's haggard face in alarm. "Goodness, honey, you look terrible! Didn't you sleep well?"

Carolyn pulled her robe tighter and walked to the table. She plopped hard into a chair and automatically reached for her mother's coffee.

"Mom," she mumbled, "something awful happened last night."

"What was it?"

"Something *awful*," Carolyn said again. "Nora was right, there *are* ghosts here. I saw Carolyn Glanton."

"What!"

"And I fell." Her voice was dull and confused, and Mrs. Baxter leaned over to pat her hand.

"What do you mean—fell out of bed?"

"No, I mean I fell down the stairs."

This time Mrs. Baxter drew back and cast a worried look toward the hall.

"These stairs? You couldn't have fallen down these stairs or I would've heard you."

"Not these stairs," Carolyn mumbled. "The attic stairs."

Her mother was looking more confused by the minute. "Attic stairs? But you can't get to the attic— that door's locked."

"No, it's not." Carolyn shook her head. "Come on. I want to show you something."

Without another word she got up and led the way to the second floor. Mrs. Baxter followed warily and stood watching while Carolyn marched straight to the end of the hall.

"It's not locked, see?" Carolyn said. "And wait till you go up there."

She yanked on the door. A strange, bewildered look came over her face, and she yanked again, harder.

"Honey, are you going to faint on me?" Mom fretted. "That door *is* locked, just like it was locked yesterday. I asked Nora about it again, but she swears up and down she doesn't know where the key is. Now, what's this about—"

"Look, Mom, all I know is, I was up there last night and something was up there with me. I fell down the stairs, and when I woke up, it was morning and I was back in my bed."

Carolyn's voice was tight and shrill. Mrs. Baxter watched her for a long moment, reached out to feel her forehead, then put an arm gently around her shoulders.

"Come have something to eat," she said firmly.

"Honey, I think you just had a bad dream. That's all. And it *seemed* real to you, and you got confused."

"No, Mom," Carolyn insisted, "that's not the way it was! I heard these strange sounds up there, and when I went to the door, it was unlocked! And there were these marks on the walls, and—and—all this blood!"

"Come on," her mother coaxed, turning her around, guiding her back to the kitchen. "Come and sit down."

"Mom, I mean it! It happened!"

"Dreams can seem awfully real," her mother said carefully. "And you've been under a lot of strain. You've been holding up for my sake, Carolyn, and I knew it was only a matter of time before—"

"Mom, listen to me—"

"Honey . . ." Mom pushed Carolyn into a chair, then knelt in front of her, taking both of Carolyn's hands in hers. She stared intently into her daughter's face, and her eyes filled with tears. "I think I can understand what you're going through. All the loss . . . the changes . . . our lives going in a whole different direction. But things are going to be better for us now. I promise."

Carolyn looked back in despair. "Mom . . . there was something up there. I *did* fall down the stairs."

"Don't you think I would've heard you? An accident like that would've made a lot of noise in the night—"

"But you were asleep in your room down here, and I was on the third floor! And the wind was howling so loud—"

"Any bruises?" Mom interrupted.

"I—no—I don't know," Carolyn said crossly. "But

I have a splitting headache. And yes, my arms are killing me. And my knees hurt." She pushed up the sleeves of her robe and pointed triumphantly to her arms. "Yes! See there? Bruises!"

"You helped me do all that moving last night," Mom reminded her. "You carried boxes up and down the stairs and rearranged some of the furniture."

Carolyn pulled away and shook her head, eyes bewildered. "It couldn't have been a dream! She stood there touching her throat—"

"Oh, that Nora," Mom muttered. "No more ghost stories. Look—I'll make you some hot chocolate, then I'll fix breakfast, and it'll seem like that bad dream never happened."

"How could it not have happened? How could it have been so real?"

"How could you have ended up in bed again," Mom teased, "unless you sleepwalked and dreamed at the same time?"

Carolyn put her hands to her face and sighed. "I don't know."

"Well, there you are. Hot chocolate coming right up."

Carolyn sat back, slowly shaking her head. She felt stiff and sore, drained and disoriented. She could still see that ghost by the widow's walk . . . those gouges and stains on the walls. . . . She could still hear those clawing sounds coming from the attic. *Mom thinks I'm going crazy. Well . . . maybe I am. . . .*

"This is crazy!" Mom shivered as she scrambled eggs at the stove. "Middle of summer and I feel like we're in the Arctic. I guess we'll get used to it." She grew quiet for a second, then gave Carolyn a sympathetic look. "We didn't really have a choice, honey. I hope you know that."

Carolyn nodded distractedly and examined the hem of her nightgown. It didn't quite touch the floor, and there weren't any stains on it.

"Carolyn?"

"I know that, Mom," Carolyn answered.

Ever since Dad's heart attack, Mom had held up amazingly, accepting with her usual grace their unexpected turn for the worse. But Carolyn knew how bad off they were financially—even though Mom tried to hide it—so when the letter had come, letting them know they'd inherited a house, it had seemed like a miracle.

"See? Your father's watching out for us," Mom had insisted when the news came about Aunt Hazel. "A fresh start for you and me. It's what we need, Carolyn. I think we should go."

Carolyn hadn't been convinced, but she'd have done anything to see her mother happy again. And now, sitting here in the kitchen, watching Mom smile over the scrambled eggs, Carolyn decided not to start the day out on a bad note. *Mom's right . . . I'm sore because of the moving . . . and I couldn't have walked around that much without waking myself up . . . and bad dreams* can *seem awfully real. . . .*

"Spit and polish," Mom said firmly. "Elbow grease."

"What?" Carolyn snapped back and forced cheerfulness into her tone.

"I said elbow grease. You heard me," Mom teased.

"Oh. In other words, you're going to work me to death."

"A good cleaning will work wonders with this place. I know we can make it charming again—I mean, it has so much potential!"

"Well . . . it has *something.*"

"Think positive, Carolyn."

"Like . . . positively awful?"

Mrs. Baxter walked over and set Carolyn's plate in front of her. "I was trying to decide . . . quilts on the beds . . . flowers on the nightstands . . . and every evening our guests could meet for hot cider and stimulating conversation in the parlor."

"As long as I don't have to be the stimulating conversationalist who gets things going."

"I really think this place could be a haven for people. You know . . . wind and cold out there in the world . . . warmth and comfort here inside our door?"

"I don't think Nora would agree with you," Carolyn grunted, making a game attempt at eating.

"Nora wouldn't agree with anything," Mrs. Baxter said. "She'd consider it unethical or sacrilegious or something. Anyway, I think Nora's interesting. It's natural for people in a small community to be leery of outsiders. And that's what we are, you know—outsiders."

"Mom . . ." Carolyn put her fork down, choosing her words carefully. "If what Nora said was true . . . you know, about people not coming over here from the mainland—then—"

"They'll come," Mom said firmly. She put her hands on her hips and nodded. "They *will.* We'll fill this old place with lots of love and"—she drew a deep breath—"they'll come."

Carolyn stared at her for a long moment. Finally she nodded.

"Okay. If you say so."

"Now, after you finish breakfast, you better get dressed. We have tons of work to do. Beginning with the dishes."

"Can't we start instead with the heater?" Carolyn pleaded. "I feel like I've been preserved in ice."

"Nora said it didn't work very well." Mom sighed. "And by the way, where *is* Nora—I thought she said she'd be here this morning by seven. I don't even know why I bothered to let the realtors know we were coming. No one did a single thing to get the house ready for us. You're right. First on our list—find someone in the village who does repairs. Oh, why didn't I pay more attention when your father was fixing things around the house? But of course I never dreamed that someday he'd—"

"I'll be right back," Carolyn cut her off and hurried upstairs.

She paused outside her room and looked at the end of the hallway. The attic door was shut, the latch in place.

She walked over and tried to turn it.

Locked.

"Sea air," she muttered to herself. "Good for the imagination, obviously."

She went into her room and pulled up the shades, frowning at the thick fog beyond the windowpanes. She had the strangest feeling that the whole house was adrift in some churning gray sea. When she'd first woken up this morning, she'd lain in bed listening to the wind and the surf, and it had taken several minutes for last night's horrors to come back to her. And then she'd thought about Captain Glanton again and the widow's walk and the shipwreck and the poor doomed sailors calling their own names . . .

"Come into the village with me." Mrs. Baxter appeared in the doorway, and Carolyn jumped. "Sorry—didn't mean to scare you!"

Carolyn gave a wan smile and shook her head. "I think I'll hang around here. Check out the new surroundings."

Mrs. Baxter glanced toward the window and nodded. "Just be careful; you heard what Nora said about the cliffs being so close. If I'm lucky, I'll bring back groceries *and* some gossip."

"If you can get anyone to talk to you," Carolyn said.

"Well, surely they can't all be like Nora." Her mother looked alarmed. "Can they?"

She didn't wait for an answer. She waved goodbye, and several minutes later Carolyn heard the front door slam.

The house surged with emptiness.

Only the whine of the wind kept her company now . . . gnawing at every crack . . . scratching at every windowpane.

Carolyn tried to shut out the desolate sounds. She stood up and began pulling clothes from her suitcase.

"You've already talked yourself into a nightmare," she grumbled. "Don't talk yourself into anything else."

She groaned when she saw what she'd brought. Shorts, mostly, and sleeveless tops and her swimsuit and two pairs of sandals. *Well, we were going to the beach, weren't we—how was I supposed to know it was the beach at the end of the world?* Irritated, she crammed her clothes into a dresser drawer and slipped into the jeans and sweatshirt she'd worn yesterday. The movers wouldn't be here for a few days, but maybe there were some clothes of Hazel's that might fit her.

It made her nervous, walking past all the sheet-shrouded bedrooms. She half expected some ancient body to be laid out on one of the beds, and every time the house creaked, her heart skipped a beat. She went through every cupboard, every trunk and armoire and bureau in record time, but didn't find anything she could wear. Hazel's wardrobe consisted of frilly, spinsterish things, and each time Carolyn pulled something out to inspect it, she felt like a little girl playing dress-up. After much searching, she finally discovered a closet beneath the staircase, but to her annoyance it only contained empty handbags, bottles of medicine, and an overpowering smell of cedar chips and mothballs.

Wrinkling her nose, Carolyn stepped back and started to shut the door, when her sleeve caught on one of the rickety shelves. She twisted around to jerk free, when without warning the whole shelf pulled away from the wall and crashed to the floor at her feet.

Carolyn surveyed the mess in dismay. Broken bottles oozed syrupy liquids across the floor, and pills scattered everywhere. She picked up the broken glass, then leaned forward to study the inside of the closet. It was obvious the wood had begun to rot away, and as she dug one finger against the ledge where the shelf had rested, Carolyn felt something small and thin buried there beneath a heavy layer of dust.

She pinched it between her fingertips and pulled it out, holding it up to the light.

A key.

At one time it must have been tossed inside where it somehow managed to slip down between the shelf and the wall, finally ending up trapped upon the narrow ledge. *No telling how long it's been there . . . or what it was used for.* Carolyn was disappointed. She started to flip it onto another shelf, when a new thought made her stop and reconsider.

A key to the attic door?

With a little thrill of excitement, she hurried upstairs and tried to force the key into the lock at the end of the hall. The fit wasn't even close, and after a few minutes of trying, Carolyn gave up and shoved the key into the pocket of her jeans. She'd have to ask Nora about it later, but right now there was work to do.

Carolyn hardly knew where to start. For several minutes she stood in the back bedroom, and then she just as grimly began yanking sheets off the furniture, tossing them out the door and into a pile in the middle of the hallway. As more antique furniture revealed itself, she shook her head and glanced down ruefully at her filthy hands.

"Hope you still believe in miracles, Mom," she grumbled, "because it's sure going to take a good one to get this house in shape."

She couldn't imagine how Hazel had lived in this place—and it was even harder to imagine how guests might actually come here and pay for the privilege of sleeping in these dark, dank rooms. Carolyn gathered up the sheets and went downstairs, making a quick detour to the parlor on her way to the kitchen.

Here—more than in any other room—she felt as if she'd taken a step back in time. The shades had come down from the windows, letting in pale, filtered light, and someone had run a dustcloth over the heavy, old-fashioned furniture so that everything gleamed with a dull shine. The rug and floorboards had been swept, and a pile of logs was stacked neatly in the fireplace. China figurines stared with chipped, painted faces. The room waited expectantly, as though a visitor from centuries past might arrive at any moment.

And maybe Carolyn Glanton stood in this same exact spot I'm standing in now and looked over at her husband while he warmed himself at the fire and told her how he was sailing away, and promised her he'd come back to her, no matter the powers of heaven and earth . . . and sea . . .

"Mom's right." Carolyn's voice was unusually loud in the silent room. "You're a hopeless, ridiculous romantic. Maybe poor Carolyn had the right idea after all. Matthew was probably a rogue and a scoundrel, and he never had the slightest intention of ever coming back for her."

With a sound of disgust, she leaned against the front door.

The pounding came right behind her head.

As Carolyn screamed and jumped away, her eyes riveted in on the upper half of the door—on a slow, dark shadow sliding across the panes of beveled glass.

Someone's trying to get in—

The pounding came again—louder this time—echoing on and on through the gloomy house. The shadow leaned forward . . . hesitated . . . then pulled back as Carolyn held her breath and frantically tried to think what to do. For one horrible second images shot through her brain—the blurry figure she'd seen outside yesterday . . . the ghost she'd seen last night in the attic—

And as she watched in growing horror, the doorknob slowly began to turn.

THE QUILTER

5

"HEY, ANYONE HOME?"

Huddled against the wall, Carolyn wasn't exactly sure what she expected to see. Certainly not the door popping open or the grocery bag thrusting into the room—and definitely not the tall young man who finally stepped across the threshold.

"Hello?" he said again. There was a long pause as he peered cautiously around the grocery sack, and then he shouted, *"Hello!"*

"Who *are* you?" Carolyn demanded furiously.

He jumped three inches off the ground. The bag fell out of his arms and spilled helter-skelter across the floor.

"What are you trying to do, scare me to death?" The young man turned on her, his voice every bit as angry as hers.

"What am *I* doing?" Carolyn forced herself to move out into the room, forced herself to sound calm, though her heart was racing out of control. "What are

36

you doing in my *house?* Get out before I call the police!"

"Well, that's just great," the boy muttered. He squatted down and began gathering up several cans of soup.

Carolyn opened her mouth, closed it again, and stared at him. After several silent moments of retrieving things, the boy finally cocked his head and looked up at her.

"Well?" he said.

"Well, what?"

"Well, are you gonna just stand there or are you gonna give me a hand?"

Carolyn kept staring. She opened her mouth once more and finally found her voice.

"Will you please leave? I think you must have the wrong house or something."

He shook his head and kept picking up groceries.

"I *know* where I am, thanks very much. You must be Carolyn."

Before she could answer, he stood up, giving her a wide friendly smile.

"I'm Andy."

He held out his hand. Taken aback, Carolyn watched as he took hers and pumped it up and down. His blue eyes crinkled and his smile widened even more.

"Andy Farrel," he added, turning her loose.

Carolyn looked down at the mess across the floor. "What are you doing in my house?"

"Bringing you these."

"I didn't order any groceries."

"I know. They're a gift."

"A gift? From who?"

"Bell's Market. In the village."

"Oh." Carolyn frowned, trying to make sense of everything. "You mean my mother had them sent over?"

"Nope. Mr. Bell had them sent over."

"Mr.—"

"Bell. He owns the market. It's a sort of welcome-to-the-island gift. And hope-you-shop-with-us gift."

"Well . . . I . . ."

His grin was disarming. "Even though you will," he said. "'Cause it's the only grocery store on the island."

Carolyn watched as he heaved the sack onto one shoulder and ambled off to the kitchen.

"Well, my mother just went to buy groceries!" Carolyn exclaimed. "Does she know about this?"

"She will soon enough. Hey, you better put the milk and juice in the fridge," Andy called back. "Or do you want me to?"

Carolyn didn't answer. She followed him into the other room as he opened a cupboard and rummaged inside. Now that his back was turned, she had time to really study him—his dark brown hair, all shaggy and windblown; tight faded jeans with one back pocket ripped across his narrow hips; faded denim shirt with sleeves rolled up past his elbows; lean arms and sinewy muscles and quick, sure movements. There was something carefree and boyish about him, and as he glanced back over his shoulder at her, Carolyn dropped her eyes.

"Haven't dusted for a while, I see. Hey, hope you

like clam chowder—he sure sent enough of it. Cheap-skate. It's not even homemade."

"Listen—Andy—whoever you are—"

"Look, this isn't my regular job, okay? It's just that I happened to be in the store when he was getting this stuff together, and he asked me if I'd run it out here." He reached for a canister on the counter, and Carolyn watched in dismay as he opened it and loaded it up with tea bags.

"Want me to make some?" he asked, but Carolyn shook her head.

"No. By all means, just keep making yourself at home."

Andy grinned again. "I brought Hazel her groceries a lot—one of my *many* odd jobs around the village. She never left her house if she could help it. Mr. Bell always said she didn't want people gawking at her. Funny old lady, Hazel. Just between you and me, I think she *liked* being the village eccentric."

He hunted in the bottom of the sack and pulled out a bag of cookies, which he promptly tossed into a drawer.

"Also from Mr. Bell. Oatmeal. Bet they're stale."

Carolyn leaned sideways against the doorframe. "You knew Hazel well?"

"Not really." Andy frowned. "She was old and old-fashioned. Blind as a bat, too. Wore these long dresses and this big hat with a veil when she walked on the cliffs. I'd see her up there sometimes when I was out in my boat."

"It sounds like you knew her."

"Knew what she looked like. Never talked to her."

"But you said you brought her groceries."

"Nora always handled that, and I talked to Nora. I'd only been working on the island a few months when Hazel died, so it's not like she and I were old friends."

He paused, stared at a loaf of bread, then shrugged his shoulders.

"I kind of wish I'd known her before, though."

"Before what?" Carolyn asked.

"Before she got so weird."

"What do you mean weird?"

Andy's face grew serious. He seemed to be groping for the right words.

"Nora told me once that Hazel was getting to be a problem. Real preoccupied and distracted. Like her mind was going—or at least going to some other world. Nora was always worrying about her."

"Was Hazel sick?" Carolyn eased down into a kitchen chair, watching as Andy bounced a bag of potato chips from one hand to the other.

"You mean physically?" He tapped the side of his head. "I think it was more up here. Nora said sometimes Hazel didn't even recognize her. And other times Hazel was scared of the house."

"The house!"

"Or scared of *something,* anyway—Nora didn't know what."

Carolyn held back a shiver. "And she never found out?"

"I think it was really starting to get to Nora." Andy's eyes twinkled. "Which is really something, considering how scary *she* is." He stopped, his voice lowering. "She's not lurking around, is she?"

Carolyn shook her head, and he sighed in relief.

"Nora said Hazel heard things that Nora couldn't hear—saw things that weren't there."

"Did she say what?"

"Voices. People walking around in the house." Andy thought a minute. "She'd see faces at the windows, or hear people on the stairs. Things like that. Or she'd ask Nora to stay over sometimes so the screams wouldn't keep her awake."

"What screams?"

Andy shrugged again. "Of course, Nora never stayed—she's always afraid she'll get possessed by something. Right—like it hasn't already happened."

Carolyn stared at him. Andy opened another cabinet and tossed the potato chips inside.

"I can't imagine anyone living out here all alone like that," Carolyn mumbled.

"Well, she wasn't always alone, I guess. Nora said Hazel took in drifters now and then—word got around the docks that she'd give them work and a hot meal. They made Nora really nervous, so Hazel would call her up and tell her not to come if one of them was staying there. Thing is, Nora never actually saw them. So who knows—maybe Hazel made them up."

"You're kidding," Carolyn said.

"No, really." He turned back to face her and crossed his heart. "Nora said Hazel would swear up and down that something was one way when it really wasn't. But you know"—his glance was almost apologetic—"old houses creak . . . old people imagine things."

He let the cupboard door slam, and Carolyn leaned toward him across the table.

41

"But what if she *wasn't* imagining it?"

Now it was Andy's turn to stare. "Excuse me?"

"What if she really *did* hear and see those things?" Carolyn burst out. "Old houses can be *haunted,* too."

"Oh." Andy's eyes narrowed. "I get it. Nora's been telling her ghost stories again. The old throat-ripped-clean-out bit. Did I forget to mention that *housekeepers* can be the most crazy of all?"

"You mean the story about the house isn't true?"

"Well, of course it's true." Andy laughed. "But Hazel lived here for years and years. So why would the spirits suddenly get restless when Hazel suddenly gets senile?"

"You don't know for sure she was senile."

"Like I don't know for sure Nora's an alien? If you ask me, those two crazy women deserved each other."

"You don't know anything about anything—" Carolyn began hotly, but Andy held up his hands in defense.

"You're right, you're right—and Hazel's your aunt, after all, so I shouldn't—"

"I didn't even know her," Carolyn grumbled. "I just happen to believe that anything is possible, and it doesn't necessarily mean you're crazy. Or senile."

Andy leaned back against the counter. She could feel his eyes on her, and she pulled nervously at a loose thread on the tablecloth.

"Okay." He nodded. "I'm open-minded."

"Is that sort of like empty-headed?"

"Ouch!" Andy's jaw dropped. "All I did was bring groceries. Okay. Let's start over."

Before Carolyn could respond, Andy started opening cupboard doors again, pulling things back out.

"Will you stop?" Carolyn watched in amazement, trying not to laugh. "I was just trying to make a point."

"Yeah. And you're about as subtle as a dumptruck."

"Well, I wasn't ever around Hazel, but I *have* been around Nora, and I really think she *believes* this place is haunted."

Now it was Andy trying not to laugh. He pressed his lips into a tight line and nodded.

"Carolyn," he said reasonably, "all the island kids think Nora's a witch. Or haven't you noticed her eyes?"

"She can't help the way she looks."

"You couldn't pay kids to come within two miles of this place! Most villagers, either, thanks to Nora's and Hazel's ghost stories!"

"I'm just trying to be fair." Carolyn looked away, embarrassed. "I think it's cruel when someone really *believes* something, and no one listens to them."

For a moment there was silence. At last she glanced over at Andy, and he smiled.

"You're right," he said. "You're absolutely right. No one will ever really know what Hazel saw or heard— not even Nora. And now Hazel's dead. So *she* can never tell us."

Carolyn's nod was halfhearted. She felt sad all of a sudden, and strangely uneasy. She wrapped her arms around herself and shivered.

"Andy . . ."

"Yeah?"

He was finishing with the groceries and glanced up from the bag. A shock of hair fell stubbornly over one eye, and he gave it an impatient swipe.

"The letter we got said Hazel died of exposure," Carolyn said. "Couldn't the doctors do anything to save her?"

"She didn't have doctors." Andy looked startled. "Nobody found her till it was too late."

"You mean . . . she died *here?* In the *house?*"

Neither of them noticed the shadow slipping along the hall outside the door. And neither of them saw the tall, dark figure glide into the room until Andy looked over and gave a yelp.

"Dammit, Nora! What is this—a conspiracy to give me a heart attack today?"

Carolyn started from her chair as Nora's eyes raked her over. In one movement the woman's black coat slid from her arms onto a chair, and she walked to the stove.

"I had to stop at the store," Nora announced crisply, putting on the teakettle. "For detergent."

Carolyn's breath came out in a rush. Andy sagged back against the counter and put his hand to his chest.

"She's the one to ask," he said irritably. "She's the one who found Hazel."

Nora stiffened. Carolyn saw the bony hands hesitate over the stove, and she could swear they trembled.

"And she didn't die in the house," Andy went on, his voice steady now. "She died out there." He jerked his chin toward the kitchen window, indicating the gray oblivion beyond.

"How awful," Carolyn murmured sympathetically to Nora's back. "I'm so sorry, Nora."

"They brought her back here and tried to revive her, but they couldn't." Andy flicked a glance in Nora's direction, but the housekeeper didn't return it. "They think maybe she'd been out there all night—maybe even most of the day before."

"It wasn't my fault!" Nora turned suddenly, her eyes flashing. "She gave me the day off! How was I to know?"

Carolyn looked back at her in surprise. "Well . . ." she stammered, "I'm sure no one blamed you. After all, if it hadn't been for you, who knows when they would have found her—"

"Wasn't the cold that killed her anyway," Nora mumbled, turning back to the stove. She snapped off the burner and set the kettle to the back. She took down a cup and saucer, china rattling softly in her hand. "Wasn't the cold at all, nor nothing like that. It was *him.*"

"Him?" Carolyn echoed.

Nora swung around, her flinty eyes holding Carolyn in a relentless stare.

"They'll say different," Nora whispered. "But me . . . *I know better!*"

6

WITHOUT ANOTHER WORD THE HOUSEKEEPER SWEPT OUT OF the room, leaving Carolyn and Andy to stare open-mouthed. After several seconds of silence, Andy finally cleared his throat.

"Well. I rest my case."

"What did she mean?" Carolyn demanded. "What did she mean by that?"

"You're asking me?" Andy feigned surprise. "This is Nora we're talking about. If you want to interrogate her, do it on your own. But not by a full moon."

"Are you afraid of her?" Carolyn asked incredulously, but Andy didn't seem at all bothered.

"Have you ever seen that movie with all those brides of Dracula?" he asked her. *"They* have eyes like Nora."

"But she seemed really upset. I'd like to know why."

Carolyn got up and crossed to the kitchen doorway, peering into the rooms beyond.

"I don't see her. Where'd she go?"

"Back in her web?" Andy suggested. "Hey, look." He hopped lightly onto the counter and sat there, long legs swinging against the bottom cabinets. The knees of his jeans were ripped out, and his sneakers were torn and stained with mud. "The first thing you're gonna have to learn is not to let Nora's wild imagination get to you. Legends are great for the tourists, but not to live with on a day-to-day basis."

"Oh, I get it. You believe in vampires, but not in ghosts. That makes a lot of sense."

Andy remained unruffled. "I realize you're trying to be Nora's good pal and all that, but hey—consider the *source!*"

Carolyn was only half listening. "Nora said something about drowned sailors. Drowned sailors calling—"

"Their own names," Andy finished. He jumped down, crossed the room in two easy strides, and poured himself some coffee. "Supposedly they call out their own names when they want the help of the living."

"And what can the living do?"

Andy shrugged and took milk from the refrigerator. He poured a thin stream into his cup before he answered.

"Help them find eternal rest."

"And how can they do that?"

"How should I know? I don't make up these legends." Andy boosted himself back onto the counter again and raised his cup to his lips. His blue eyes squinted mischievously at her over the rim.

"You're making that up," Carolyn grumbled.

"Hey, I wouldn't do that."

"And you don't really believe *that* story, either." She lifted her chin indignantly while Andy grinned.

"One legend's as good as another, as far as I'm concerned. With all the rocks and cliffs along the coast, this has always been one of the most dangerous islands—put that with the wind and fog, there're only a few spots around here a boat can safely land. It's not the best atmosphere for happy endings, you know what I mean? So the island stories have lots of murders and suicides in them. Not to mention pirates . . . smugglers . . . hurricanes . . . shipwrecks . . . you name it, it's had them all."

"So what," she challenged him, "if none of them are true?"

Andy sipped his coffee. He gazed thoughtfully into his cup, and then he grinned.

"Ever hear of ghost lights?"

"No." Carolyn poured herself some coffee and tried to sound bored.

"Lots of people claim they've seen them. Spooky lights glowing down along the water late at night. Some say it's a natural phenomenon—weird gases coming out of the rocks when the atmosphere's just right. But others say the lights are the souls of drowned sailors. And that the sailors can't rest till they're reunited with what they loved most in life."

In spite of her coffee Carolyn shivered. "You're making fun of me. You don't believe it."

"Hazel did. Nora does."

"So you think I'm a crazy eccentric just like them." Carolyn sniffed. "Thanks a lot."

She went to the sink and rinsed her cup. Andy's grin widened.

"Pretty eyes," he said.

"What?"

"I said," he repeated, hopping lightly to his feet, "you have pretty eyes."

Carolyn glanced at him, feeling a flush across her cheeks. "Stop it."

"Come on, can't you take a compliment?"

"They're not pretty," she said, flustered.

"They have that nice shape," Andy went on, his own eyes sweeping her casually. "Kind of wide and innocent. Even though I bet you're not. Innocent, I mean. Not that you're wide, either. Actually, you're pretty tiny."

Carolyn opened her mouth, but stopped short of an angry reply. Instead she laughed helplessly.

"I'm trying to be mad at you!"

"Don't try. You won't be able to do it."

She flushed again and sat back down at the kitchen table, watching as he sat across from her.

"Well, I already know you're from Ohio," Andy said amicably, scooting his chair sideways, crossing his long legs. "And I already know you're here for a business venture. But that's about all the information I've been able to dig up so far."

"I don't know what else to tell you," Carolyn said truthfully. "Hazel's really a long-lost relative on my mom's side of the family. My dad died suddenly, and then my mom found out she'd inherited this place. So we decided to come and . . . you know . . . start over."

She glanced up into his blue eyes. This time when he smiled, there was unmistakable kindness.

"I'm sorry, Carolyn. This must be hard for you."

"I hated to come," she admitted. "But Mom really wanted to. So for her sake . . ."

To Carolyn's surprise Andy reached across the table and squeezed her hand.

"Look, if there's anything I can do . . ."

She shook her head, not knowing what to say. "I didn't mean to go on like that. I hate it when people expect you to listen to all their problems."

"I'm a good listener."

He still had ahold of her hand. Carolyn fidgeted and tried to change the subject.

"So . . . do you get many tourists out here?" she asked, and Andy smoothly followed her lead, releasing her at last.

"Lots in the village. But on this side of the island . . ." He sighed and shook his head. "Have you had time to look around yet?"

"No. It was kind of late when we got in last night."

"It's not Ohio, I'll tell you that. As a matter of fact, I don't think it'll be anything like you're used to."

"That much I've figured out." Carolyn gave a shudder. "It's so . . . *depressing*. The wind sounds so sad."

"It never stops blowing," Andy informed her. "Not out here, anyway, and some days you wonder if you'll ever see the sun again. It's always darker and colder— but beautiful, too, in its own way. A wild kind of freedom, I guess."

"So you come out here often?"

"Only by water. When I take my boat out."

"Your boat?"

He nodded and smiled. "I take tourists around. Another of my many odd jobs. Fishing . . . sightseeing . . . whatever. Or sometimes I just go by myself. To be alone. To think."

"So is that all? Delivering groceries and riding around in your boat?" Carolyn tried to keep a straight face as Andy leaned toward her.

"No. Sometimes I go out. You know . . . on dates. With girls. Who aren't sarcastic." He grinned and raised an eyebrow. "Everyone's saying you'll never pull this off, you know."

"Pull what off?" Carolyn looked surprised.

"Making a profit off this place. Turning it into something . . . you know. Interesting."

Carolyn sat straight in her chair. "They don't know us very well! *And* they underestimate our determination!"

"And just *who* do you think would ever come out here to stay?" Andy settled back again, a triumphant grin on his face. "It's too far away from anything except water."

"Well . . . water lovers, then!" Carolyn blurted. "People who enjoy having a little privacy from the rest of the world. Like you in your little boat."

Andy cracked up. As Carolyn realized she'd fallen into his trap, she didn't know whether to laugh or hit him. As if anticipating her second choice, Andy stretched to his full height and moved out into the parlor.

"It's freezing in here, Carolyn. You can't depend on

Nora to keep the fire going—don't you know reptiles are cold-blooded?"

Before Carolyn could answer, he took down a box of matches from the mantel, then knelt on the hearth to rearrange the wood in the fireplace. Moments later smoke was curling up the chimney, and Carolyn held her hands gratefully to the flames.

"I know you think I'm silly," she said at last, "but there really is something about this house that fascinates me."

"Fascinates?" Andy teased. "Or scares?"

Carolyn didn't laugh. "I don't know . . . maybe a little of both."

"Well, maybe if you're lucky, you'll manage to see a ghost or two while you're here."

Carolyn stiffened. She opened her mouth to tell Andy about her nightmare, then changed her mind and gazed into the fire.

"Wouldn't there be something written about it somewhere?" she asked softly. "Old journals or newspaper articles or pictures or something?"

"What?"

"For"—Carolyn thought quickly—"for the brochure."

Andy looked lost. "What brochure?"

"You know. For the house. For the guests."

"Oh. Something to stir up tourism." He glanced at her, thinking. "You might find something in the library."

"There's a library?"

"Halfway up Main Street. I don't know how good it is, though."

"You've never been there?"

"I don't have time to read." He looked shocked. "I'm too busy delivering groceries and riding around in my little boat."

In spite of herself, Carolyn laughed. She knelt beside him on the hearth and leaned in close to the crackling flames. Overhead the ceiling creaked softly as Nora's precise, measured steps went back and forth between the upstairs rooms. Andy cocked his head, jerking his chin toward the floor above them.

"So you're keeping Nora."

"Mom wants to." Carolyn sighed. "She'll need help once I start school, and Nora's worked here so long, Mom didn't feel it was right to let her go."

"How do *you* feel about it?"

Carolyn hesitated before she spoke. "Andy, what Nora said earlier—about how Hazel died—"

"Oh, come on now. I told you, everyone knows Nora's crazy."

"But what if she's not? She said Hazel was *killed*. And she talked as if she knew who did it."

"If you're gonna start listening to Nora's gloom and doom, you'd better pack up and move right back to Ohio, 'cause she'll have you spooked in no time." Andy raised an eyebrow, his tone suddenly serious. "Hazel died from the cold. Doc Brown thinks she must have lost her balance, and when she fell she couldn't get back up again. She'd been lying out there all night in the wind and rain, and she was old. That's all there is to it. Nora's just trying to get to you. She's never gonna accept the fact that you and your mom are living here now instead of Hazel."

Carolyn was quiet a long moment. "She really loved her, didn't she?"

"Loved her?" Andy made a sound in his throat and concentrated on tossing more kindling into the fire. "One thing you can say about Nora. When she's committed to something, she's extremely dedicated."

"Poor thing," Carolyn murmured. "Maybe it's a good thing Mom kept her. She's probably so lonely now."

Andy leaned over and ruffled her hair.

"Got to go. Don't want to wear out my welcome."

He stood and went to the door, and Carolyn jumped up to follow.

"Wait," she called after him. "Do you know which room it was?"

Andy looked blank. He opened the door, hunching his shoulders against a blast of raw wind. "Did I miss part of this conversation?"

"The murder," Carolyn said. "Which room was it in?"

Andy hesitated. Then he slowly crooked his finger, motioning her to come closer. As she came up beside him, he leaned over and lowered his voice.

"Which room are you sleeping in?"

Carolyn's eyes widened. "The room to the left of the stairs. On the second floor."

"That's it, then." Andy nodded solemnly. "I'm sure that's the room where everyone got slaughtered."

"Andy—" Carolyn began in exasperation, but he put a finger to her lips and shook his head.

"Repeat after me. Nora is a fiend. I will not listen to Nora's stories ever, ever again."

He laughed as he hopped off the porch and hurried to his car.

And even though Carolyn slammed the door after him, something cold and sinister hung in the air, as though an uninvited guest had entered and decided to stay.

7

FOR A LONG TIME CAROLYN STOOD THERE.

For a long time she stood by the door and even wished Andy was with her again—talking, laughing, smiling that mischievous smile—anything to break the awful stillness of the house.

"I will not listen to Nora's stories ever, ever again. . . ."

But Andy hadn't been in the attic last night— hadn't seen the dripping walls . . . hadn't seen that horrible thing floating there in the fog . . .

"Stop," Carolyn whispered. "It was just a dream."

She shuddered and turned around. Nora was standing right behind her, and as Carolyn stifled a scream, the woman turned and disappeared into the darkness of the hall.

"Andy!"

Flinging open the door, Carolyn ran out onto the porch, frantically searching the drive and the narrow dirt road that led back to the village.

Not a soul in sight.

Nothing to break the desolation that stretched endlessly around her.

Carolyn gritted her teeth against the wind. Then she ducked her head and hurried away from the house.

The fog was beginning to lift. Somewhere beyond the gray scudding clouds, a faint glow of sun was burning off the last few hours of morning, and Carolyn scanned the horizon with hopeful eyes. Mist clung to her cheeks and lashes, wetting her hair to her face. The sound of the sea echoed like thunder all around her, and she could taste salt in the air.

"She keeps watch for him . . . and he searches for her . . ."

"It's a house for the dead . . . not the living . . ."

Carolyn stumbled, catching herself before she fell. Just ahead she could see a break in the fog, and she hurried toward it.

And then without warning, the voice came.

"Maaaatthewwwww . . ."

Carolyn froze, her heart lurching into her throat.

A voice?

Or only the wind?

It came once, but did not come again. It floated from nowhere, from fog and from shadows—a deep voice, choked thick with water, a voice that held both rage and unmistakable terror.

It was the most horrible, most unearthly sound she had ever heard.

"Who's there!" she screamed.

The wind whipped her words away, almost before they were spoken. *I will not listen to Nora's stories—I will not listen—*

She pushed her way through the fog, when suddenly her foot began to slide. Scrambling for balance, Carolyn teetered forward and saw the edge of the cliff beneath her shoes.

The earth shifted and crumbled.

In desperation Carolyn flung herself backward onto solid ground and lay there, gasping for breath.

One more step . . .

One more step and she would have walked off into nothingness.

Shaking violently, Carolyn craned her neck forward to get a better view. Far below, jagged rocks gleamed black and wet with foam, rising up from crashing waves and shadowy pockets of sand. Gulls shrieked and circled overhead, and like silent sentinels, more outcroppings of deadly rocks camouflaged themselves beneath the tumbling rush of the sea.

It took several minutes to calm herself down . . . several more before she remembered the voice.

"They call out their own names when they want the help of the living . . ."

Carolyn got to her feet and gazed at the scenery around her. She could see the hazy sky and the endless cliffs and the ocean going on and on forever. . . .

"I imagined it," she said fiercely. "It was just the wind . . . just the birds."

The gulls screamed in reply, mimicking her, going round and round in slow, maddening circles.

Carolyn stood there, gazing down, down on the wide, curving beach. Her heart had slowed to its normal rhythm again, and she slowly unclenched her hands.

There was a way down—she could see it now, just

barely—a crude sort of path carved into the adjacent cliff wall. She followed it with her eyes all the way to the bottom, where it finally gave out onto a little cove.

I can't keep being afraid of this place if I'm going to have to live here.

Everything could be easily explained, if she just took time to think it all through. She still had Nora's ghost stories on the brain. She hadn't been watching where she was going, even though Nora had warned her about the cliffs.

Again Carolyn forced herself to look down at the cove. *Is that where Nora found Hazel? Is that where Captain Glanton and his whole crew drowned?*

"It was a knife he took . . . and chopped off the captain's hand. . . ."

Carolyn closed her eyes, and for one moment she actually thought she could see it—just how it had happened that horrible night. The handsome young captain half drowned, clinging desperately to the slippery rocks, one arm wounded, and the other arm—his stronger arm—stretched out to the one person he believed would help him. Of course he couldn't have known. Of course he couldn't have suspected that the one man who could save him wanted him dead. And so Matthew Glanton had reached out to a stranger—and there had been one dull blow—and at first he probably hadn't even realized what was happening as he lost his hold on the rocks . . . as he slipped back into the churning waves for the last time. . . .

Carolyn opened her eyes. There were tears on her cheeks, and she wiped them away. *What's the matter with you—you are so pathetic!*

She began walking farther along the cliffs, trying to peer into the shadows and hidden places far below. Andy had said that nobody ever came out to this end of the island, and now she could certainly understand why.

"No self-respecting ghost would be caught dead in a gloomy place like this," Carolyn whispered to herself, and laughed softly at her own joke.

Then suddenly she saw him.

And at first she tried to tell herself it was just a trick of the light—some feeble ray of sunshine reflecting off the dull sheen of the sea, wavering ghostlike among the misshapen rocks and chunks of driftwood scattered across the sand. . . .

Carolyn blinked her eyes and squinted, trying to focus in on the silent, distant figure in the shadows.

She'd seen it once before.

Outside the window, and only last evening . . .

Her breath caught in her throat. A slow, icy chill crept through her, and her heart hammered out of control.

You're imagining things again! There's no one there!

Yet every nerve screamed inside her, every instinct told her to turn, to run, as hidden eyes—*human eyes*—watched her from below.

"No," Carolyn whispered to herself, and then louder, *"No!"* and she *did* turn then, and she ran, away from the cliffs where the invisible eyes couldn't follow. She ran faster, and she kept looking back over her shoulder, but there was nobody there—*nothing!*—only the desolate cliffs and the hazy sky and the mournful call of the sea.

She pounded up the front steps and into the house,

slamming the door behind her. And then she leaned against it and shut her eyes, her whole body shaking with deep, ragged breaths.

She didn't notice the movement in the corner.

Didn't realize anything was even wrong until the tall shadow pulled itself from the gloom and moved noiselessly toward her across the floor.

Carolyn saw his stare—the gleam of his eyes—but she couldn't scream, couldn't even move, as his hand lifted slowly to her arm.

His touch was as cold as ice.

As cold as death itself.

"I need a room," the stranger said softly. "I'll be staying awhile."

8

CAROLYN KNEW HER MOUTH WAS OPEN—COULD FEEL THE scream lodged there at the back of her throat—but she couldn't seem to do anything—move, breathe—or even answer. Instead every sense was focused in sharply on the tall, dark-haired stranger standing before her.

His shoulders were broad, his body lean but well-built. He wore a sleeveless vest with no shirt underneath, and there was a skull tattooed over one tanned bicep. A tiny gold hoop hung from his left ear. His jeans were tight, his hair long and wavy, and dark brows drew low over the blackest, most piercing eyes Carolyn had ever seen.

In some remote part of her brain she felt the front door pushing against her. The next second, it shoved her forward and Mrs. Baxter stumbled into the room, catching her balance as she glanced from Carolyn to the young man and back again.

"Hello," she said pleasantly. "Carolyn, why on earth didn't you help with the door—didn't you hear me yelling?"

Carolyn simply stared.

"Mom—" she said hoarsely, but Mrs. Baxter was already shrugging out of her jacket, unwinding the scarf from her head. She walked over and took the stranger's hand, pumping it warmly.

"Hi there, I'm Merriam Baxter—we just moved in. My goodness, you're freezing! Come over here by the fire and get warm—Carolyn, honey, you'll never guess. There's some kind of festival going on in the village this weekend! Isn't that great?"

"Mom," Carolyn tried again, but her mother didn't hear.

"Are you from the village?" she chattered on, while the young man continued to stand and watch them. "What kind of a festival is it, anyway, do you know?"

"I need a room," he said quietly, and this time Mrs. Baxter stopped talking and leaned closer, not certain she'd heard him.

"A room?" She sounded bewildered. "Here? *Now?*"

"I don't have any money," he went on. "But I think we can help each other."

And they were both staring at him—both Carolyn and her mother—and Mrs. Baxter's mouth dropped open an inch.

"Each other—*how?*" Then she shook her head and laughed. "You'll have to forgive me, I'm a little confused. I thought you said—"

"I heard you needed help around the place." He made a vague gesture. His fingers were long; his

63

movements graceful. "To get ready for tourists. I can do anything you want. I'll help you get the house in shape if you let me use one of your rooms."

Mrs. Baxter was looking more bewildered by the second. Beside her, Carolyn shifted and grabbed her mother's arm.

"Uh, Mom—can I talk to you a minute? In *private*—"

"I don't think I got your name. . . ." Mrs. Baxter began politely, and the young man stepped forward to take her hand.

"Joss," he answered, and his eyes shifted smoothly to Carolyn . . . back again to her mother. "Joss Whitcomb."

"Mr. Whitcomb—"

"Joss."

"Yes." Mom nodded and flushed slightly at his handshake. "Well . . ."

"Mom," Carolyn said again, but her mother moved toward the fireplace. She stared into the flames, and then she smiled at Joss.

"Are you from the village?"

"Just passing through."

"How long were you planning to stay?"

"As long as it takes."

"Mom . . ." Carolyn said through clenched teeth, but Mrs. Baxter didn't seem to hear.

"You see it, too, don't you?" Mom was positively beaming. "The potential of this old house? What it could be with some loving care? I just *know* it was magnificent in its day. And it can be again, I think."

Joss smiled and said nothing.

"Well, you look strong enough," Mrs. Baxter added,

"though you could use a little more meat on your bones. When was the last time you ate?"

"Mom—"

"Carolyn, go in and start lunch, why don't you? It must be this awful wind out here—I'm starving, and I know our guest must be, too!"

Carolyn stared helplessly while her mother sat down and motioned Joss to do the same.

"Is this a hobby of yours?" Mrs. Baxter asked him. "Rebuilding old monstrosities?"

A faint smile touched his lips. They were full and perfectly shaped. He wore no beard or mustache, yet a shadow traced along his upper lip and darkened the sharp contours of his chin.

"Let's just say . . . I admire beautiful things." Again his eyes shifted to Carolyn, and she quickly looked away.

Mrs. Baxter clapped her hands together. "Oh, how rude of me, I'm so sorry! Joss, this is my daughter, Carolyn."

Carolyn mumbled a welcome as his steady gaze traveled slowly from her head to her feet. Carolyn found it unsettlingly hypnotic.

"She's going to be a senior this year." Mom went on before Carolyn could stop her. "We just moved from Ohio—the woman who used to own this house was my great-aunt."

Joss inclined his head politely.

"I lost my husband not long ago, you see," Mrs. Baxter said. "So now it's just Carolyn and I."

"Only the two of you?" Joss repeated slowly.

Oh, Mom, why'd you tell him that—why'd you tell him how terribly alone we are—

"Well . . . and Nora, of course," Mrs. Baxter added. "She's our housekeeper. We sort of inherited her from Aunt Hazel."

"I'm sorry about your husband," Joss said, and his voice was very soft, very deep. "Maybe it's good I'm here."

Mrs. Baxter mulled this over. At last she smiled. "Yes. Yes, I think it might be."

"*Please*, Mom"—Carolyn made a quick gesture toward the kitchen door—"I really need to talk to you."

"What is it, Carolyn? Can't it wait a minute?"

"Don't mind me," Joss said. "Go ahead."

"I'll be right back," Mrs. Baxter promised, and then as she glanced toward the hallway, "Oh, come in, Nora. Meet our first real guest, Joss Whitcomb."

Joss stood up, but as Nora came slowly into the room, a puzzled look went over his face.

"Not ready for guests," Nora sniffed. "He'll just have to make do."

"It's not a problem, Nora." Mrs. Baxter sighed. "Joss is going to help us out for a while, doing repairs around the house."

"This is Nora?" Joss sounded so funny that Mrs. Baxter turned to him in surprise.

"Why, yes. Hazel's housekeeper I was telling you about."

Nora's eyes narrowed suspiciously, but Joss didn't seem to notice.

"Then who's the other woman?" he asked.

As everyone turned to stare at him, he gestured toward the front of the house.

"The one I saw when I came in," he added.

Mrs. Baxter shook her head. "I don't know who you mean. There's no one out here but us."

"But she was standing up there," he insisted quietly. "Up on the widow's—"

He broke off as the tray Nora was carrying crashed to the floor.

"No," Nora whispered, and her hands fluttered feebly to her throat as though she couldn't breathe—*"No!"*

She took a step backward, into the shadows.

And before anyone could move, her body crumpled to the floor.

9

"Nora!" Mrs. Baxter cried. "Oh, dear, put her here on the couch! Carolyn, quick, call a doctor!"

Carolyn watched helplessly as Joss carried Nora back to the parlor. In black dress and shawl and stockings, the housekeeper resembled some grotesque stain spreading across the horsehair sofa.

"Carolyn, *now!*" Mrs. Baxter ordered.

Carolyn hurried to the phone. She lifted the receiver and started to dial, but a strong hand closed firmly over hers. Startled, she looked up into Joss's eyes.

"There's no need for that," he said quietly.

Carolyn's heart raced. She couldn't take her eyes from his. A muscle clenched in his jaw, and he pulled the phone away, replacing it on the table.

"Carolyn, will you please—" Mom broke off as Joss knelt beside the couch. He pressed his hand to Nora's forehead, massaging gently. Almost at once the housekeeper's eyes fluttered open.

"She'll be all right," Joss said.

He stood and moved back. He leaned casually against the mantel, and Mom stared at him in dismay.

"Nora?" Mom patted the woman's cheek, slipping one arm beneath her back to prop her up.

At first Nora didn't seem to remember anything. Her eyes darted from Mrs. Baxter to Carolyn and then around the room, finally coming to rest on Joss.

"Nora, wake up," Mom coaxed. "You fainted, that's all. You scared us all silly."

Nora had regained a little color, though she still looked pinched and strained. She pulled out of Mrs. Baxter's grasp and got slowly to her feet, and by the time she was standing again, she'd managed to perfectly recompose her face.

"I don't need any help," she said coldly. She was staring hard at Mrs. Baxter, her eyes never once straying to Joss. "But *you* will. *All* of you will, mark my words."

"Oh, Nora, for heaven's sake—"

"My mistake," Joss said so suddenly that once again everyone else in the room turned to stare at him. "It must have just been a shadow or something. I didn't mean to upset everyone."

"That was no shadow," Nora murmured, and at last Carolyn spoke up.

"Then who was it, Nora? The captain's wife? But how can you be sure? It *could* have been a shadow—"

"Of course it was a shadow," Mom broke in impatiently. "What on earth else could it have been? Have you eaten, Nora?" When the woman maintained a sulky silence, she added, "Carolyn, make sure you fix Nora something for lunch, too."

"I'm perfectly all right," Nora insisted, but her

voice was barely a whisper, and Carolyn noticed how her hands were shaking. Catching Carolyn's stare, Nora clasped her fingers together and stiffened even more.

"Forgive us, Joss," Mrs. Baxter said with forced brightness. "We're not usually quite this neurotic around here. The truth is, we've all been through a pretty rough time recently, but now things are going to be much better. Right?"

The room grew quiet.

Lifting her eyes, Nora stole a reluctant glance at Joss's face, then turned and went straight to the kitchen.

"Poor Nora." Mrs. Baxter sighed and shook her head. "I don't think she's in very good health, and I'm afraid she's still so upset over Hazel's death. She was devoted to my aunt, you see."

"How touching," Joss murmured.

Carolyn excused herself and followed Nora into the other room, but before she could strike up a conversation, Mrs. Baxter joined them there.

"Nora, are you really all right? I know you have certain . . . ideas and such about the house, but I wish you wouldn't share them with the guests—at least not before they've had a chance to settle in. Heaven only knows what he's thinking."

In answer, Nora started banging pots and pans on the stove. Carolyn darted a quick look at her before she spoke.

"Maybe he did see something, Mom. It could happen."

"What he saw was a shadow—much to his regret, I'm very sure."

Mrs. Baxter rolled her eyes in exasperation, took a long, deep breath, then let it out again, a sure sign that she was on to more important matters.

"Carolyn, are you thinking what I'm thinking?" She burst into a big smile. "He's the answer to our prayers!" When Carolyn didn't respond, she stopped and studied her daughter's face. "So why are you looking like that?"

"I don't know," Carolyn said, busying herself at the counter. She really *didn't* know—she felt all mixed up inside. She opened a container of chowder that Andy had brought and shrugged her shoulders. "This guy's a total stranger, Mom."

"Well, really, Carolyn, this isn't exactly like the neighborhood we just moved from. People here still leave their doors unlocked. They trust each other."

"Who told you that?"

"Some of the people I talked with this morning in the village. They're all so nice and *wonderful* people! Like that Mr. Bell sending groceries."

"It's just"—Carolyn groped for words—"strange, don't you think?"

"What is? What do you mean?"

"Showing up the way he did, just when we needed someone to help us."

"Drifter," Nora muttered, and they both looked at her.

"What was that, Nora?" Mom asked.

But if Nora heard, she gave no sign. She turned on the tap water so hard that the pipes groaned.

"But that's what makes it so wonderful, Carolyn!" Mrs. Baxter raised her voice above the noise. "It's like we're destined to succeed with this place, don't you see? We needed help—and here's help!"

Carolyn glanced at Nora. The housekeeper stood stiffly at the sink and kept her back to them. She seemed to have forgotten the dishes entirely. Now she picked up a long-handled knife, ran one finger slowly along the blade, and started slicing a loaf of bread.

"Carolyn," Mrs. Baxter went on, "if you're going to start nitpicking, then this little coincidence should make you feel *good* about being here. Like someone's watching over us. Nora, look, the sink's starting to overflow—"

Carolyn frowned. "You want him to stay?"

"Well, of course I want him to stay! Nora, did you hear me about the sink? We need the help, Carolyn! Don't *you* want him to stay?"

Carolyn looked at her mother's hopeful face.

No, she wanted to shout, *no I want him to leave, I want him to leave right now, right this very second— because suddenly I'm feeling really scared and I don't know why—*

The water shut off. The room grew quiet.

"Yes," Carolyn mumbled. "Okay, Mom. I want him to stay."

"Then hurry up with lunch, will you? What is that, anyway?"

"Clam chowder. It's part of the stuff Mr. Bell sent over."

"Isn't that sweet!" Mrs. Baxter started to leave, then paused in the doorway to look back. "I can't *believe* the friendliness and generosity of these people! I met Mr. Bell when I was out shopping this morning, and he was so *nice* to me—let me open an account right away! Then he introduced me to some of the other people who came in—and they showed me where different stores were—and they told me where to shop for what—"

"Can't you find out something about him?" Carolyn fixed her mother with a pleading look.

"Who?" Mrs. Baxter looked baffled. "Mr. Bell?"

"No, that guy in our living room. Before he stays?"

"Carolyn, do I have to remind you that the guests who'll be staying here will all be people we don't know? And if you're going to be concerned with running a check on each and every one of them, I guarantee we'll *never* have anybody staying! That's not how you run a guest house!"

Carolyn shook her head, trying to make her mother understand, though she didn't even understand herself.

"He was waiting inside when I got back from my walk. He was standing in the parlor. Like he *belonged* here."

"Well, the poor boy was practically frozen—did you want him to wait outside till he died of pneumonia?"

"Mom, he saw someone on the widow's walk!"

"Thought he saw someone. Just like you *thought* you fell down the attic stairs last night! For heaven's sake, Carolyn, anyone can be fooled by a shadow. Quit being so suspicious. I thought you wanted this to work."

"I . . . I do . . ."

Their eyes locked. Mrs. Baxter shook her head impatiently, her voice tight.

"Carolyn, we have *no* income. There was *no* life

insurance. Your father, bless his heart, totally supported my being a homemaker, so I don't know how to do *anything* else. This opportunity came along, and I took it. I'm doing the best I can."

A flush went over Carolyn's cheeks. She looked away and nodded slowly.

"I'm sorry, Mom. You're right. Things are different now."

"Honey," Mrs. Baxter said, moving to Carolyn's side, tilting her daughter's face up, "we desperately need help around here—Joss needs a place to sleep. Let's just accept the little gifts that come our way and not question them, okay?"

Carolyn managed a weak smile. "Okay, Mom."

She watched her mother leave the room, and then she glanced over at Nora. During the whole conversation Nora had been slicing that same loaf of bread— sawing the knife slowly back and forth against the cutting board.

"Are you all right, Nora?" Carolyn asked, but the woman's shoulders remained just as stiff, just as straight.

The knife made a dull thudding sound as Nora laid it on the counter.

"Nora?" Carolyn tried again. "Joss was telling the truth, wasn't he? There really *was* someone up there on the walk, and he really did see her."

Nora didn't turn. Her right hand made a quick swipe at her apron, then closed around the knife again.

The blade sawed once.

"I've cut myself," Nora said.

Carolyn rushed to her side, seeing the dark red flow over Nora's wrist. She turned on the faucet and forced Nora's hand beneath the water, then looked anxiously into the woman's face.

It was a perfect mask. No pain . . . no surprise . . . nothing.

"Clumsy of me," Nora mumbled.

"Nora—"

"It's only a scratch. I'll tend to it in the bathroom."

Before Carolyn could answer, Nora turned away and disappeared down the hall. Carolyn heard the bathroom door close, and she leaned against the counter, putting her head in her hands.

"Carolyn!" Mrs. Baxter called.

"Yes, it's almost ready!"

She could hear them talking as she heated the soup, as she toasted the bread, as she ladled the chowder into bowls and arranged places at the kitchen table. Mom's voice always got louder when she was happy, and she was certainly happy now.

"It seemed like such a perfect opportunity when I got this place," Mrs. Baxter was saying as she and Joss strolled into the kitchen. "I've always wanted to open a guest house—and it was a good time for making changes."

Carolyn leaned over to check a burner on the stove. She felt Joss pass behind her . . . felt his body lightly brush against hers. She straightened, a funny feeling in the pit of her stomach.

"Well, you'd think with this being our first guest, we could at least eat in the dining room," Mom teased, waving Joss into a chair.

"This is fine," Joss assured her. "Very homey."

Carolyn served the soup and bread. "Does anyone need anything else?" she asked politely.

"Sit down and join us," Mom said.

Reluctantly Carolyn pulled up a chair, but she didn't feel like eating.

"Carolyn could certainly use a friend," Mrs. Baxter went on softly. "This move has been especially hard on her. Leaving all her old friends behind—"

"Mom," Carolyn broke in quickly, "I'm sure all our problems are really boring to him—"

"We're only getting acquainted." Mom sounded a little annoyed at the criticism. "And I'm sure Joss must know that awful feeling of having to leave people behind, traveling around like he does."

The black eyes shifted to Carolyn's face.

"I've had to leave lots of people behind," Joss said quietly. "And you could never be boring to me, Carolyn."

Carolyn looked away, flustered. *What is he doing here? Why is she letting him stay?*

"As a matter of fact," Joss went on, dropping his eyes, studying his soup spoon, "I feel like I know you already."

The room seemed to grow smaller around her— smaller—and smaller still—until there was just her and Joss and the echo of his voice in the silence and the sheen of his hair as it hung dark and loose around his face—and then his eyes lifted again—slowly— and she was caught there—trapped—something foreign and frightening and terribly wonderful fluttering deep, deep in her heart—

"—Carolyn?"

"Wh-what?" Carolyn stammered.

Her cheeks went pink as she realized everyone was staring at her. Even Nora, who had managed to slip back into the kitchen and was now lurking in a corner near the window.

"Daydreaming again," Mom teased, and Joss smiled, flashing perfect white teeth. "I said when Joss is finished, why don't you take him upstairs and let him have his pick of the rooms."

Carolyn nodded and pushed back from the table, hardly aware that Mom was still talking.

"I'm afraid they're all rather musty and damp. We only moved in yesterday, like I said, and we really weren't even planning on opening for another—"

"I'd like a front view," Joss broke in. "Is that possible?"

Mrs. Baxter nodded. "Of course. The room right across from Carolyn."

Again Joss's eyes slid smoothly to Carolyn's face, and for one crazy second she had the weirdest feeling that he already *knew* where her room was.

He smiled. "Perfect."

"So in case you need anything—" Mrs. Baxter began, and Joss leaned forward, nodding.

"Yes. In case I need anything, I'll have Carolyn."

Carolyn stared at him. Then she looked at her mother, but Mrs. Baxter was leaning back in her chair now, going on as though she'd known Joss for years. She glanced at Nora, but the housekeeper was gazing out the window and seemed strangely removed from both kitchen and conversation. Mrs. Baxter patted Carolyn's arm and motioned her to get up.

"Why don't you go on upstairs? There're fresh

sheets and blankets in that closet outside the bath-room. Joss, I'll turn you over to Carolyn, but promise you'll let us know if there's anything else we can do for you."

He didn't say anything as Carolyn led him to the second floor. They moved together through the murky halls, and Joss paused in each doorway, looking in, nodding to himself. The rooms felt clammy and chilled. As they passed Carolyn's, Joss stopped. For a long moment he gazed in, then finally he looked at her.

"Something happened in this house," he said.

Carolyn stiffened slightly. She gave what she hoped was a casual nod. "It's an old house. I imagine lots of things happened here."

"I mean something sad. Something . . . tragic."

Carolyn shrugged. "Well . . . Hazel died, of course —she's the one who used to live—"

"No," he said softly. "Not Hazel. And besides, your mother already told me she didn't die in the house."

Carolyn kept her eyes on the floor. "I don't know what you mean."

She could feel him staring at her. She could feel herself getting nervous and flustered, and she strug-gled to keep her face expressionless.

"It's a feeling I get," he murmured. "About houses. They're a lot like people, really. They have emotions. They have secrets."

She still didn't raise her eyes.

"I've heard stories about the house," she mumbled at last. "But I don't know how true they are."

"Well," he said softly. "Maybe we'll find out."

He moved away from her, catlike footsteps fading down the corridor.

"Ah," she heard him say, "the way to the widow's walk."

Carolyn's head came up. She turned to see him standing beside the attic door.

"How did you know that?" she demanded.

"Lots of old houses were built this way," Joss said calmly.

"It doesn't have a key."

"Good. We wouldn't want anyone getting hurt. It looked like it was in pretty bad shape from outside."

Carolyn said nothing. He walked back toward her, and she instinctively stepped out of his way.

"The room over there," Joss announced and pointed to the door across from hers. "Is that mine? You don't have to bother with the bed—I can make it up myself."

Carolyn hesitated. She watched as he opened the door of the linen closet. He took out sheets and a blanket and two pillowcases. He smiled at her over his shoulder.

"Maybe you better take more blankets," she said grudgingly. She wished he wouldn't smile at her, it made her nervous. "That room's colder than the others. The windows rattle all the time."

"It's the north corner," he said.

"Well . . . I'll help you with your suitcase. Where is it?"

"I don't have one."

She'd started down the stairs, but now she stopped and looked back at him.

"You're traveling, but you don't have a suitcase?"

"It was stolen."

She felt herself nod as if this were perfectly normal. She heard herself say, "Then I'll have to find you some clothes, I guess."

"I can get some in the village later on."

"Well . . . there probably wouldn't be much around here you could wear anyway—"

"Don't worry," Joss said. "I have everything I need."

He walked into his room.

Carolyn caught a glimpse of his smile, and then the door shut between them.

10

"MOM, I'VE GOT TO TALK TO YOU ABOUT—"

"What, Carolyn?"

"About—"

"What, honey? I can't hear you! All that noise!"

Carolyn halted in the kitchen doorway, rubbing sleep from her eyes. She'd almost been afraid to go to bed last night, what with Joss in the house and the memory of her attic experience still fresh in her mind. But the night had been blessedly uneventful, and she'd slept like a rock. Now Mom was sitting at the table with papers strewn around her, scribbling on a tablet, while somewhere outside a steady sound of hammering vibrated the walls and floors.

"The brochure?" Mom yelled. She barely noticed as Carolyn sat down.

"What brochure?"

"*Our* brochure," Mom said, pencil between her teeth. "Of course it'll have the name and address and rates and special features. But we should include points of interest, don't you think? Special things tourists might want to do while they're here."

"You mean freeze to death? Stumble in the fog and fall off a cliff? Commit suicide from severe depression?"

"Stop being dramatic, Carolyn."

"Okay, how about go deaf?"

"That's why Joss is here—to fix things. Goodness, you're grumpy this morning."

"I'm not grumpy, I'm realistic. This place isn't Disneyland, Mom, or haven't you noticed?"

"Maybe if you could go into the village for me," Mom went on, undaunted. "See it through fresh new eyes. What would attract you to come here, to want to stay in our guesthouse. Then we need to decide where to advertise. I've already thought of the stores here, but what about on the mainland—hospitals, universities, travel agencies, and—"

"Joss bothers me."

"Does he?" Mom glanced up in alarm. "What'd he do?"

"Oh, I don't mean that. I mean he just . . . well . . . *bothers* me."

Mom threw her a sly look. "I think he's kind of cute."

He's very cute, Carolyn thought grudgingly. *He's more than cute. He's handsome . . . mysterious . . .*

"He's . . . different." *Can't you see it, Mom, can't you feel it—he's not like other people—*

"Carolyn, you're not going to be on intimate terms with every guest who checks into our house. At least, I certainly hope not."

"Mom, come on—"

"Just do me this one favor today, okay? Just go into the village and make a list of all the interesting things to see and do."

Sighing, Carolyn got up and started toward the front door. "Where are your keys?"

"I'd rather you walked."

"Walked!"

"Well, for goodness' sake, Carolyn, it's only a few miles, and the sun's out. I want you to notice the *scenery!*"

"What scenery?"

"We need to describe our guest house in some sort of . . . you know—enticing environment. As a matter of fact, that has a nice ring to it, don't you think? Enticing environment." She mumbled it to herself several more times and smiled. "So try to notice what's around you—"

"Fog."

"And how it smells—"

"Like fish."

"And colors—"

"Gray."

"And impressions—"

"Horrible."

"Really, Carolyn, this attitude of yours isn't getting us anywhere."

Carolyn slammed the front door and stomped off, not slowing down until she was a good quarter mile down the road.

Then she thought about Joss.

She thought about his dark eyes, and his rugged looks, and the tiny gold hoop on his earlobe . . .

Like a sailor, she thought. *Just like a sailor might wear.*

She stooped down and picked up a handful of pebbles. She drew back her arm and let them fly, watching as they sailed up and up into the pale morning sky and then rained down again into a field of scrubby grass.

"A drifter, he was, looking for work. And she needed the help of a man around, and so she let him stay on . . ."

"Ghosts," Carolyn whispered to herself. "Impossible."

And yet Joss had seen a woman on the widow's walk when he'd come to the house. *Even though it could have been a shadow. . . .*

And she had witnessed a bloody scene in the attic. *Even though it was probably just a nightmare. . . .*

And there had been that strange, unearthly voice calling through the fog. *Even though it was probably just the wind. . . .*

A gull shrieked overhead, startling her back to reality. Carolyn watched it soar and circle out beyond the cliffs, and she envied its freedom. Squaring her shoulders, she walked on, even smiling a little as the sun warmed and brightened. Overhead the last gray clouds dissolved, and she tilted her head back and let her hair blow free.

She purposely avoided looking down as she rounded a sharp bend in the road—a place where the cliffs crowded dangerously close on the left. Shading her eyes, she peered into the distance and saw sails billowing out on the water, waves sparkling, birds reeling through the bright blue sky. Off to her right lay dark, tangled treelines and crumbling stone walls and an occasional cottage with smoke curling lazily above a shingled roof. From somewhere came the muffled bleating of sheep . . . the anxious bark of a dog. But still, the sea was ever-present—its salty taste filling the air, its steady pulse pounding and echoing on and on in all directions.

Carolyn suddenly realized that her *own* heart was beating in time to the sea, and she stopped on the road and let her eyes wander slowly in the direction of the cliffs. She could see a narrow ridge jutting out farther than the others, and she chose this spot to peer down over the side.

The wind was stronger here than on the road, whipping her hair about her face, stinging her cheeks with fine spray. Squinting, she gazed far, far out across the water—miles and miles of bottomless ocean. The coastline lay like a giant serpent, coiling back and forth between bare stretches of sand and walls of craggy rock. To Carolyn's surprise she saw a familiar rooftop silhouetted faintly in the distance, and she realized it was Glanton House. From this vantage point she could see how frighteningly close it really was to the cliffs. Like something shunned and alone . . . perched precariously at the very edge of the world.

Suppressing a shiver, Carolyn turned away. She picked up her pace and was relieved when the village came into view at last.

The festival was in full swing. Booths had been set up in streets and on sidewalks, on corners and in yards, even on the village square. Bright awnings flapped in the breeze, and every imaginable craft and ware were on display. Carolyn could smell the tantalizing aroma of food, and she suddenly realized how hungry she was. She felt in her pocket for money and decided to sightsee awhile.

The narrow streets had been blocked to traffic—instead of cars, they were packed with people. Carolyn bought a hot dog and wandered up and down cobbled lanes and shaded alleyways, stopping from time to time to browse through shops or peek into busy cafés. Antique dealers were everywhere, alongside art galleries and musty bookstores. Artists had set up easels along the sidewalks and were happily painting beneath bright beach umbrellas. At the lower end of Main Street, Carolyn could see a dock crowded with boats and fishermen, while at the opposite end the street rose steeply up a hill, ending at an old stone church. She finished her hot dog, threw the paper into a litter can, and started up the incline.

She found the library about halfway up the hill, just as Andy had told her. The place was practically empty, the front desk deserted, and the only person Carolyn could see was a raggedy woman sitting at a table in back.

"Excuse me," Carolyn whispered, easing up beside her. "I was wondering—would you have any information on Glanton House?"

An old wrinkled face looked up at her. Silvery hair splayed out stiffly in all directions, and watery gray eyes appraised her with one sidelong glance.

"Glanton House?" the old woman rasped. "And why would you be so interested in Glanton House?"

"I'm Carolyn Baxter, and I'm going to be living there now. Hazel was my—"

"Bad end," the woman said solemnly, and Carolyn's eyes widened.

"Excuse me?"

"Bad end!" the woman hissed. "Hazel met a bad end! Everyone who lives there—sooner or later—comes to a bad end!"

Carolyn glanced uneasily around the room. She still couldn't see anyone, yet she had a nagging feeling that they were being listened to.

"What do you mean?" she asked softly. "About the bad end?"

The old woman stared. Her huge eyes bugged out, reminding Carolyn of a fish, and when she patted the chair beside her, Carolyn could see that she was wearing a pair of gloves with the fingers cut out.

"Tell me," the old woman lowered her voice, motioning Carolyn to lean close. "Do you think I'm crazy?"

Carolyn pulled back, startled. "Well . . . I don't even know you—"

"But if you *did,*" the old woman insisted, and her eyes narrowed suspiciously, "would you think I'm a little off? Just because I'm Molly McClure and people say Molly McClure is touched in the head? Just because I *know* what I *know?*"

Carolyn shook her head slowly. "I've never even heard of Molly McClure. What *do* you know?"

"Sit down," the woman said.

"But—"

"Sit *down.* Here. Beside me."

Carolyn sat. She would have preferred to sit at the other end of the table, but Molly McClure had ahold of her arm and was pinning it to the tabletop.

"Glanton House," the old woman mumbled. "Strange things going on there . . . even now."

"What kinds of strange things?"

"Him."

"You mean . . . Captain Glanton?"

"Ah, so you *do* know something about the house!" Molly's eyes grew even larger, as though they would burst right out of her head.

"I've heard a little," Carolyn admitted. "From Nora."

"Nora," the woman snorted. "Now, *she's* crazy!"

"But you were saying," Carolyn reminded her, "about Captain Glanton?"

"Coming back to kill that faithless wife of his! Coming back for all eternity, and the killing never stops! That's true love for you!"

Carolyn's mind was racing to keep up. "Wait—you say *the captain* came back to kill his wife? But how do you know it was him? I thought Carolyn's lover was missing, and the murderer was never caught—"

Carolyn broke off as Molly snatched her hand and squeezed it tightly. The old woman's voice was a hoarse, dramatic whisper, and she rolled her eyes toward the ceiling as she talked.

"That stormy night, Matthew's hand was cut off, wasn't it, my girl? And he slipped straight into the sea, never to be seen again. But Molly McClure has her own ideas about what happened. Molly McClure thinks our poor captain *lived* through that horrible night and vowed to get even. But first, he had to get back what was taken from him."

"You mean"—Carolyn swallowed hard—"his wife?"

"Not his wife. His *hand,* girl. His *hand.*"

Carolyn looked confused. "But I don't see——"

"Oh, and he got it back all right, the scoundrel!" Molly's eyes rolled wildly. "He had them fasten a *hook* right onto that bloody stump! And then he stole into Glanton House one dark, dark night and *ripped* Carolyn and that lover of hers to *bits!*"

Carolyn could hear Molly's voice, but suddenly it seemed like a long way off, and the room was throbbing around her. . . .

Something clawing . . . scraping the walls . . .

"No," Carolyn murmured.

"Spilled their guts all over the room! Bloodbath, it was!"

Scratches on the walls—splatters on the floor—

Carolyn shook her head, trying to clear it. "I guess lots of people have their own theories about what happened that night——"

"My theory is, he cut that lover of hers into fishbait! And that's why he was never found!"

"But I guess no one will ever really know," Carolyn finished weakly. The room had grown very hot, and she fanned herself with one hand.

"By the water at night—I *see* things. Straaange things . . . chill-your-blood things." Molly's voice sank . . . trembled. She put her lips close to Carolyn's ear. "Shadows over Glanton House. Ghost lights on the beach! It's *his* beach, it is—and *his* house still! And does the captain ever find what he's looking for? Hmmm . . ."

To Carolyn's dismay Molly pulled back and dug both hands into the silvery mats of her hair.

"Does he find what he's looking for?" she mumbled

again. "No . . . no . . . or else he'd go away now, wouldn't he? Or else he'd go back to where he came from. . . ."

"Molly," Carolyn said slowly, "what are you talking about?"

"He *should* go away. He doesn't belong here now. What can it mean but more grief? What can it mean but more tragedy?"

Molly closed her eyes, covering them with her hands. Then, as Carolyn watched nervously, she slowly lowered her hands again and folded them in her lap.

"You think I'm crazy," she muttered.

"No," Carolyn said quickly. "No—no, I really don't—"

"When the key to the whole problem is so simple."

"Simple?"

"All you have to do is find it."

"Then tell me what you mean, so I can."

"The captain will tell you." Molly's toothless grin was slow and sly. "If you just listen to him."

"But . . ." Carolyn was growing more frustrated by the second. "If he's dead, then how can I—"

"Know him for what he *was*," Molly hissed at her. "And then . . . you will know things for what they *are*."

To Carolyn's surprise the old woman rose abruptly from her chair.

"Don't stay," she murmured, pointing a gnarled finger in Carolyn's face. "Bad house . . . bad end."

She turned her back. Walking barefoot and trailing

a shopping bag behind her, she staggered around the table and out the front door.

Carolyn sat and stared.

She rubbed the chill from her arms and glanced nervously around the empty room.

Well, this is just great. I come in for some basic information, and I end up in the Twilight Zone.

"Can I help you find something?"

The voice was so close that Carolyn jumped, knocking a stack of books onto the floor. Embarrassed, she bent to retrieve them while the pleasant-faced woman behind her knelt down to help.

"Oh, here, don't bother," the woman scolded gently. "I have to put these back on the shelves anyway."

"Gosh, I'm so sorry—"

"Don't be. I see you met our Molly—she tends to have the same effect on most folks when they're first introduced." The woman laughed softly and stood back up, balancing the books easily in one arm.

"Oh . . . I wondered," Carolyn babbled, "I thought maybe she was the librarian or something."

"Or something, is right." The woman laughed again. "No, *I'm* the librarian and if I hadn't been buried in the stacks back there, I'd have heard you come in." She gave Carolyn a quick handshake. "Jean Lawford. Molly just comes in here to read from time to time. She can't afford books of her own—or a house, either, for that matter."

Carolyn stared at the door where Molly had gone through. "Where does she live, then?"

"Mostly on the beach. She sets up housekeeping in

some of the old caves down there . . . walks up and down all day, picking up litter and generally scavenging. According to her, she's found some real treasures." Jean smiled and shifted the books from one arm to the other. "Don't let her upset you. She's not well, poor thing. Doc Brown manages to get medicine to her, but whether she takes it or not . . ."

"You mean, you can't really tell?" Carolyn guessed.

Jean shrugged and flashed a smile. "Let's just say that when she *does* take it, it confuses her even more. Poor old Molly never makes sense—to herself or anyone else."

Carolyn smiled and sat back down. "We were talking about Glanton House."

"Hmmm . . . well, I can show you what I've got, but understand, most of it's hearsay. Legends and superstitions and scary campfire stories."

"My mother and I are living at Glanton House now. We're going to make a guest house out of it," Carolyn went on, and was pleased to see Jean's nod of encouragement.

"Isn't that wonderful! Then you'll need something for a little PR—but more positive than scary, am I right?"

Carolyn gave her a grateful smile. "Anything would help."

They both looked up as the door burst open. Carolyn saw the tall figure hurrying toward them, but it took her a few seconds to realize it was Andy.

"Carolyn . . ."

He stopped beside her chair, and she knew something had happened—knew it by the look on his face and the sudden fear in her own heart. She got slowly to her feet and felt Andy take both of her hands in his.

"What is it?" she mumbled. "What's wrong?"

His eyes held hers, steady but sympathetic.

"It's your mother," he said gently. "There's been an accident."

11

"I'M GOING TO TAKE YOU HOME," ANDY SAID.

Carolyn nodded, but things weren't quite registering. She stared hard into Andy's face, searching for answers behind his words.

"Is Mom okay?" she finally whispered, and Andy's hands were on her shoulders now, squeezing tightly. He looked like he'd rather be anywhere else in the world but here.

"She took a bad fall," he told her carefully. "Someone called from your house, and Doc Brown rushed right over. Whoever it was said you'd come into the village, and could someone try and find you."

"I've got to go." Carolyn turned helplessly toward Jean, but the librarian was already shooing them out the door.

"Bless your heart, good luck to you!" she called.

Carolyn looked back to thank her, but Andy was already hurrying through the crowds.

"Come on," he said urgently. "We'll take my car."

Carolyn couldn't think. She was only vaguely aware of the crowds streaming past, of climbing into a car, of weaving through narrow streets until at last they cleared the village and headed out onto the cliff road.

The windows were down, and the stiff sea air bit fiercely at her cheeks. After several moments Carolyn felt revived enough to look at Andy beside her. His jaw was clenched, and his brows drew worriedly over his eyes.

"How bad is she hurt?" Carolyn asked.

"I don't know any details, Carolyn, I just—"

"Well, who called?"

Andy gave her a sidelong glance as he swerved to miss a hole in the road. "I don't know. Some guy. He said he lives there."

"Lives there!" Carolyn exclaimed. Her mind raced furiously, and she groaned. "He doesn't live there—well, I guess he *sort* of lives there—"

"What are you talking about?"

"His name is Joss. He's boarding with us. He's doing odd jobs, and Mom's letting him stay for free."

"When did that happen?"

"Yesterday after you left. He just showed up."

"What do you mean, he just showed up?"

"I mean I was out for a walk, and when I got back, he was waiting inside the house. Like he belonged there."

Andy frowned. "How did he know about you? You're not even open yet."

"He said he'd asked around in the village. Mom was totally charmed by him."

"And you weren't?"

Carolyn thought of those black eyes . . . the broad shoulders . . . the deep voice . . .

"He's just some drifter," she said. "He won't be there forever."

Andy didn't say anything, and Carolyn rushed on.

"Didn't he tell you what happened? Didn't he say anything about how she is?"

Andy shook his head. "I didn't talk to him. I don't know anything else."

"Then how did *you* find out about it? How did he know where to call?"

"He didn't. He called 911 and told them what had happened and said someone needed to find you. I guess Nora told him that I knew you, so the dispatcher phoned down to the dock and got ahold of me."

Carolyn stared at him. "How did you know where I was?"

His smile was quick and warm. He reached over and squeezed her hand.

"I figured, being the determined girl you are, that you'd head straight for that library."

Carolyn gave a wan smile. She turned back to her window and tried to concentrate on the scenery so she wouldn't have to focus on other, more upsetting things. Like what Mom could possibly have been doing to have an accident. And how long had she lain there before Joss found her and called for help.

Oh, Mom . . . this can't be happening. . . .

She thought about Hazel lying helplessly out in the wind and rain. She thought about Molly McClure's weird ramblings, and then with a shuddering breath,

Carolyn blanked out her mind so she wouldn't have to think anymore.

"Here we are," Andy announced, slamming on the brakes. "Looks like the ambulance beat us."

Carolyn jumped out. She ran up the front steps and into the parlor, bracing herself for the worst.

They were standing in the dining room—Joss and Nora and an elderly man in suspenders—all talking quietly. As Carolyn and Andy came in, Nora pressed a handkerchief to her nose, and the man gave a solemn nod. Joss walked silently to the window and leaned against the sill.

"Where's Mom?" Carolyn demanded. "How is she?"

Joss stared at her. The man mumbled something to Andy that Carolyn couldn't hear, then took a step toward her and put a hand on her arm.

"This is Doc Brown," Andy introduced her.

His smile was kind but serious. "Sit down, Carolyn."

"No!" Carolyn nearly screamed at him. "Where's my mother?"

"She took a bad fall." Doc Brown was talking slowly, as if Carolyn were a small child. "She's unconscious right now, and she's lost a lot of blood."

"But—but how—"

"She cut herself when she fell," Doc interrupted. "She's got some pretty nasty bruises, and till we can examine her more closely, I'm not ruling out the possibility of internal injuries. That's why I'm sending her over to the mainland. There's an excellent hospital there, and I want to keep her a few days."

The room went spinning. For an endless moment, wind seemed to fill the house with wild, panicky screams.

"I want to see her," Carolyn mumbled. "Where is she?"

That wind—why doesn't it stop—bad house—bad end . . .

"—sit down," someone was saying, and there were hands on her arms, on her shoulders, guiding her to a chair, pushing her into it.

"—shock," someone else was talking now, and Carolyn looked around at the four faces with her in the room. Andy and Doc were watching her with wary expressions. Nora blended into the shadows of the hallway. Joss's arms were folded across his chest, his eyes narrowed to black slits. He had no expression at all.

"I want to see her," Carolyn mumbled again.

Before anyone could answer, there was a commotion from the stairs. Carolyn jumped up and ran over, just in time to meet the stretcher coming down.

"Mom?" her voice broke, and she was hardly aware of Joss beside her, trying to hold her back. "What happened, Mom? Can you hear me?"

"She can't," Joss said quietly. "She fell off a ladder in one of the bedrooms. She must have hit the dresser on her way down and broken the mirror."

"Oh, my God . . ."

The stretcher was in full view now, and as the paramedics guided it toward the door, Carolyn stared in horror at her mother's face. If it hadn't been for all the blood, Mom would have looked as if she were sleeping.

"Mom?" Carolyn choked. "Mom, can you hear me?"

"She's unconscious," Doc said again.

"I'm going with her." Carolyn followed the stretcher to the front door, but Doctor Brown put a restraining hand on her arm.

"There's nothing you can do, Carolyn. Why don't you just stay here and—"

But Carolyn pushed past him out onto the porch. "I'm going with her."

"Right," Andy said quickly. "We'll follow in my car."

Carolyn gave him a grateful smile. She hurried down the steps after him, then suddenly remembered the house.

"Nora—" She stopped and turned around. The housekeeper was standing by the front door, her heavy black shawl fluttering around her bony shoulders. Perched there on the top step, she reminded Carolyn of a black crow. "Nora, would you mind—"

"Won't do any good," Nora mumbled, tucking her hands beneath the folds of her shawl, gazing solemnly down at Carolyn.

"What won't?" Carolyn retorted sharply. "What are you talking about? Can you stay and look after the house till I get back?"

"Won't matter one bit," the housekeeper's voice dropped even more. "Not even if she pulls through this time."

"What do you mean *this* time?" Carolyn demanded. "Nora?"

But Nora swept down the steps past her, leaving a

cold chill in her wake. Carolyn watched her walk off in the direction of the road. Nora didn't look back.

"Where's she going?" Carolyn turned helplessly to Andy. "What's *happening?*"

"Don't worry about the house," Joss said quietly. She'd almost forgotten he was there.

At the sound of his voice, Carolyn looked back at the porch. Joss was framed there in the doorway, his eyes narrowed and watchful.

"Don't worry about the house," he said again. "That's what I'm here for."

12

"YOU CAN'T STAY WITH HER," ANDY SAID FOR THE HUN-dredth time. "There's nothing you can do, and she's getting the best care she can get."

Carolyn sighed and leaned across the table. The hospital coffee shop was practically empty, and her fourth strong refill sat in front of her, cold and untasted.

"Oh, Andy, I'm just so worried—"

"I know you are. But she woke up, didn't she? And she talked to you, so that's another good thing. And she acted like she knew you when they let you go in."

Carolyn gave a reluctant nod. "I told her I wanted to get a motel room so I could be close to her."

"What'd she say?"

"She said no. Then she said 'house.'"

"Which means . . ."

"Knowing Mom, it means she wants me to go back and finish fixing it up."

Andy smiled gently.

"She has a one-track mind, you know," Carolyn tried to joke. "Even on her deathbed, she'd still be worried about that stupid guest house."

"She's not on her deathbed," Andy said. "Don't talk like that. She'll be fine."

Carolyn looked at him hopefully, and he smiled again.

"And then she said 'paper,'" Carolyn went on.

"Paper?"

"I don't know. I guess because we were talking about advertising this morning when I left the house. She wants to put ads for the guest house in all the papers."

Andy raised his cup to his lips, watching her over the rim.

"And then she said 'Joss,'" Carolyn added.

Andy's eyes narrowed. "And what does that mean?"

"I don't know." Carolyn frowned and shook her head. "I just thought—knowing Mom again—that she wanted me to make sure he was taken care of. She's so thrilled about him being our first guest and all."

Andy swirled his coffee in his cup. "Sure. That's probably it. Did your mom mention Nora?"

Carolyn thought a moment. She'd had such a short time with her mother in the recovery room, and Mom's speech had been so garbled, that she'd only been able to recognize a few words of their conversation.

"No," she said, "I'm pretty sure she didn't say anything about Nora." She gazed at Andy, who avoided her eyes. Then she said slowly, "I guess she'll want Joss to stay on and finish the house."

"I guess."

Carolyn looked down at the tabletop. Her head ached and she slowly rubbed her temples.

"Maybe Nora will stay with you," Andy said softly.

Carolyn looked up with a weak smile. "Is mind reader another of your odd jobs on the island?"

He shrugged sheepishly. "You just look worried, that's all."

"I'm just wondering . . ."

"What?"

"I don't know. Why she said Joss's name, I guess."

"I thought you had that figured out."

"I don't know," she said again. Something dark seemed to be nagging at the corners of her mind, but she was too exhausted to deal with it.

"So . . . what are you gonna do?" Andy asked her, and Carolyn sighed.

"I want to be with Mom, but I can't afford a motel. And I can't just run off and abandon the house—and I can't just leave it with strangers."

"Nora's not a stranger."

"And Nora would never stay there, you know that as well as I do. Mom's counting on me to hold things together while she's gone."

Andy toyed with the handle of his cup. He gazed down at the plastic tablecloth and traced over a stain with his fingertip.

"Anyway, I shouldn't mind so much being alone with Joss, should I? I mean, there're going to be lots of times I'll be alone in the house with just the guests. It's not a big deal."

"Who are you trying to convince?"

"It's not," Carolyn said again firmly. "It's really no big deal."

"It is if you're uncomfortable about it," Andy corrected her. "And somehow I think you're uncomfortable about it."

Carolyn opened her mouth . . . said nothing . . . shut it again.

"It's just that he"—she looked frustrated, searching for words—"he's so *strange*. So . . . so . . . *there.*"

"There?" Andy raised an eyebrow.

"Yes. You know . . . he has this presence. Don't you get a weird feeling from him?"

Andy shook his head, deadpan. "I hardly know the guy. And anyway, he's not my type."

"Andy, I'm serious!"

"Okay, okay, I'm sorry. Look, I admit, I'm not a hundred percent comfortable about you staying there alone with him—but I'm not sure if it's only 'cause I know *you're* uncomfortable about it, or if it's 'cause . . ."

"What?"

"Well . . ." Andy fidgeted with his cup again . . . straightened in his chair . . . crumpled a napkin in his fist. "You know. Just 'cause he's a guy."

"You're not making sense."

"You're right. Forget it."

Andy leaned back in his chair and crossed his arms over his chest. In his grubby jeans and torn white T-shirt he looked more boyish than ever, and Carolyn smiled as she noticed a smudge of dirt across his forehead and down one cheek.

"The truth of the situation is," Andy said reasonably, "he's a guest and you're the hostess. He's the handyman, and you're the boss."

"He also saved my mother's life," Carolyn reminded him.

Andy stared at her. He seemed to mull this over, then gave a noncommittal shrug.

"Well, he did, didn't he?" Carolyn persisted. "He's the one who called 911 and told them to find me. Even though," she added graciously, *"you're* the one who really found me."

Andy seemed deep in thought. He moved his lips slightly, as though talking to himself, and then he shook his head.

"I can't argue with that," he said at last.

"But what? What are you thinking?"

"I'm thinking . . ." Again Andy started to speak . . . hesitated . . . then said, "I'm thinking I better get you home."

"There *must* be a way I can stay with Mom," Carolyn groaned, and Andy shook his head in gentle reprimand.

"The doctor doesn't want her having visitors for a while. You heard him."

"Yes, I heard him," she conceded glumly.

"Carolyn"—Andy chuckled—"she's going to be fine. Now, stop worrying!" He looked relieved as Carolyn tried to smile. "Look, why don't you go home and get a good night's sleep, and tomorrow, if the doctor says it's okay, I'll drive you back here. In fact, I'll bring you back every day, if you like. Anytime he says you can come."

"That's really sweet of you, Andy. But that's asking a lot."

"You didn't ask. I volunteered."

He swallowed the last of his coffee, stood up, and nudged her toward the door. As they walked out of the coffee shop, Andy suddenly stopped in his tracks, slapping his forehead with his palm.

"Damn—I really *do* have to get back to the island. I totally forgot—I'm taking some tourists on a boat ride tonight. Hey, why don't you come with me?"

Again Carolyn smiled but shook her head. "Some other time maybe. I'm not exactly in the mood for tourists."

"But are you in the mood for the tour guide?"

"Let's get back. You've been so great about all this—"

"Hey"—he grinned at her—"I'll do anything to get out of work."

"Even be with me?" she teased.

"Especially be with you. As a matter of fact, I think you could easily become my most favorite excuse."

She had to laugh at that. After checking with Mom's nurse one more time, they went out to the car and headed for home.

Twilight was falling. As the last few rays of a brilliant sunset sank slowly beneath the sea, the world went shadowy and still. Carolyn stared out her open window, then closed her eyes, letting the salty night air wash over her face and mingle with her tears.

"What else can happen?" she murmured.

"What?"

"I said, what else can happen? Hazel died, and now Mom had an accident. And you say you don't believe in haunted houses." She thought about the attic and the voice on the cliffs, and she wanted to tell him, to talk about it, but suddenly she was just too tired.

"Why don't you try to sleep?" Andy suggested. "I'll wake you when we get home."

For a long time Carolyn was silent. Then she glanced at Andy's profile and said, "Before you found me in the library today, I was talking to Molly McClure."

"Who?" Andy sounded puzzled.

"Molly McClure," Carolyn said again. "And she was telling me her theory about the captain."

"Oh, no," Andy groaned. "The hook. Okay. Now I know who you mean. The bag lady who wanders around the beach all day getting drunk."

"She's not drunk," Carolyn corrected him. "She's sick."

"Right."

"No, really. The librarian told me that Doctor Brown gives medicine to Molly because she's sick, and the medicine makes her confused."

"Okay." Andy smiled. "If you say so."

"Why didn't you mention the hook before?" Carolyn's tone was mildly accusing. "It's horrible, but it's a really good theory. It makes a lot of sense."

"I guess." Andy sighed. "If you believe ghost stories make sense."

"She said a lot of weird things. Things that—well—actually, most of them *didn't* make a whole lot of sense."

Andy glanced over at her. "Like what?"

"I don't know . . . she sort of rambled on and on. She talked about the hook and how the captain was a murderer. And she warned me about staying at the house."

She had Andy's full attention now. He glanced at her again and frowned.

"I hope you're not gonna let someone like that scare you."

"She said she sees strange things—shadows in the house and ghost lights by the water. And she said things about the captain, too, but they were all mixed up and I really didn't understand a lot of it."

Andy shook his head slowly. "She probably *does* see strange things if she's drunk—uh, sorry—*medicated* all the time."

"She said he isn't finding what he's looking for or else he'd go away. And then she said he'd tell me things if I listened to him."

Andy rolled his eyes. "That's great, Carolyn. Is she planning on having a seance by the sea?"

"She told me to . . ." Carolyn closed her eyes, thinking back, trying to recall every word. "To know him for what he was, and then I'd know things for what they are." She opened her eyes again and shrugged. "Something like that."

Andy threw her a sidelong glance, then slowly shook his head. "Doesn't make a bit of sense to me, either, Carolyn. Sorry."

"But don't you see? Molly warned me about the house! She said things about more tragedies happening, and I could tell she really believed it. She was scared."

"Carolyn"—Andy gave a tolerant sigh—"after what the librarian told you about Molly, please explain to me why you're even listening to those stories!

So what does this mean? The captain's ghost is on the rampage? He pushed your mom off a ladder?"

"Maybe."

Andy made a sound in his throat, but Carolyn rushed on.

"Listen—the other night I heard something moving around over my room. Something was hitting the wall and then sort of scraping it. It was so—so—" She broke off, feeling that same panic she'd felt then. "It was horrible! I was so scared! I'll never forget those sounds as long as I live!"

"Mice," Andy said reasonably. "Or rats. Or bats, even. Old houses are full of them—especially the attic."

"Well, Mom tried to convince me I dreamed it. But I didn't." Carolyn turned to him with a stubborn frown. "I *didn't*, Andy! Something was up there! I saw it!"

"What do you mean, you saw it? Saw what?"

"When I went up, it looked like blood all over and I saw—"

"Shadows, probably, or old stains. Geez, Carolyn, the house is over a hundred years old!"

He kept his eyes on the road. His jaw clenched slightly, and it was several seconds before he spoke.

"You know that couldn't be real, don't you. You know that couldn't have happened."

"But it did happen!" she insisted. "When I went out in the hall, the attic door was *open*. But it's never been open before, and Nora said there's no key."

She started to say more when something nagged at the back of her mind. Andy was talking again, but Carolyn frowned, searching back through her memory. *Key . . . of course . . . that key I found yesterday in the closet . . .*

"Andy—"

"—but doors are pretty common symbols in dreams, aren't they?" Andy was going on, and Carolyn realized she'd missed half of what he'd been saying. "Maybe the doors mean something. You know, making choices. Making changes. Discoveries. Uh . . . transitions . . . going from one place to another. Things like that."

Carolyn pulled herself back to the conversation, shaking her head adamantly. "I went upstairs, and then I saw a ghost—well, something—by the door that goes out to the widow's walk—"

"Well, there, you see?" Andy said triumphantly. "Another door!"

"Listen, Andy, that door was the least of my worries, okay? There were *gouges* in the wall. Deep places where the wood was scraped away. And there were these dark spots splattered all over everything, and a pool of blood coming across the floor. Don't look at me like that—I know what I saw! And then when I was talking to Molly today, she told me about the hook. And it makes sense, Andy, it really does!"

Andy groaned. *"What* makes sense? Certainly not you at this particular moment—"

"The captain was in a jealous rage. He murdered Carolyn, then chopped up her lover. He clawed the walls with his hook and got bloodstains all over the place and—"

"Listen to you!" Andy's jaw dropped. "I think you're beginning to enjoy this, Carolyn. And you really think, after all these years, that no one ever bothered to straighten up the attic or wash away the blood?"

"Why would they?" Carolyn threw back at him. "People were scared of everything in those days. After a brutal murder like that, they probably avoided the house like the plague!"

Andy opened his mouth to argue, but Carolyn kept on.

"And remember the voices, Andy?"

"What voices?"

"The voices of the drowned sailors calling their own names? Well, I heard one yesterday—I swear I did! Along the cliffs by the house. He was calling Matthew!"

Andy's glance was patronizing. "And you'd swear to it—*swear to it*—that it wasn't the wind or the gulls?"

"Well . . ."

"For God's sake, Carolyn, where do you think these legends come from? Those superstitious people you were just talking about didn't have rational explanations for spooky noises, so they made things up!"

Carolyn stared at him, a sinking feeling in the pit of her stomach. She wished more than anything that she'd never told him about any of it.

"I know what I saw," she said sulkily.

Andy chewed his bottom lip. He put one hand to his forehead and pushed back his hair.

"I'm not debating what you saw in the attic, okay? I think you probably saw everything you say you did— but in a dream, not in real life! And I know how eerie those gulls sound out there on the point—it can make your skin crawl. At least think about it, Carolyn.

You've been under a whole lot of stress, and Nora's been filling your head with all her gory stories."

"I saw that stuff in the attic," Carolyn said through clenched teeth.

"Oh, yeah? Okay, then, fine. Just show it to me when we get to the house."

"I can't."

"Why not?"

Carolyn's look was almost sheepish. "Because when I woke up, the door was locked again. That's why Mom said I dreamed it. But look—" She pushed up her sleeve, and Andy leaned over, squinting.

"What's that?"

"Bruises."

"I can't see them. Are you sure they're not shadows?"

Carolyn stiffened and yanked her sleeve in place again. "If you don't believe me, then wait and look again when we're in the light."

She heard Andy chuckle softly, but when he reached to touch her shoulder, she pulled away.

"Well, it might interest you to know that when I was trying to get out of the attic, I also fell. No, I don't think I fell, I think something *pushed* me. All the way down the steps. That's the last thing I remember till I woke up in bed the next morning. This bruise," she said smugly, "is evidence."

"Carolyn," Andy said patiently, "how many boxes did you lug around that day? How many times did you go up and down the steps and run into things?"

"You sound like Mom," she accused him.

"Well, your mom is sensible. Like *I'm* trying to be sensible. You *dreamed* it! There's no other explanation except for something supernatural, and I don't see why some ghost would suddenly decide to come back to Glanton House *now*. Hazel lived there all those years and—"

"She saw and heard things that nobody else did!"

"Okay, okay. I get the message."

"Maybe she saw ghosts, too. Carolyn watching . . . the captain searching . . ."

Andy gave a solemn nod. "The lover loving . . ."

"Andy!"

"Sorry."

Carolyn didn't think he looked sorry at all, and she turned her attention back out the window.

They were almost to the house now. As Andy pulled off the main road down the long narrow drive, Carolyn could feel her heart hammering, her muscles beginning to tense. Glanton House loomed before her, forbidding and alone. Only one window showed any light. Andy turned off the engine, and almost at once they saw the front door open.

Carolyn didn't move. She waited as the tall figure glided through the shadows along the porch . . . watched as it came slowly down the stairs and toward the car.

"Who's that?" Andy mumbled.

"Joss. You met him earlier."

"I didn't actually meet him, Carolyn. I mean, it wasn't like we were introduced or had time for socializing—"

"Well, then, you can meet him now."

"He moves like a ghost, Carolyn. What's wrong with him—doesn't he have feet?"

Any other time Carolyn might have found this

funny, but now as she watched Joss move closer, she felt only a growing uneasiness.

"Carolyn," Joss said. He stopped on Andy's side and leaned in through the window. "How's your mother?"

The wind was blowing, and it was hard to hear. Carolyn watched Joss's dark hair stream wildly back from his face.

"She's going to be okay, I think." Carolyn swallowed over a lump in her throat. "She woke up before I left, and we talked for a little while."

"That's a relief," Joss mumbled. "Nora made dinner, and I kept it hot. I thought you'd want something to eat when you got home."

"I'm not very hungry," Carolyn admitted.

Andy glanced over at her and asked, a little too loudly, "Is Nora staying tonight?"

"No," Joss said. "She was just getting ready to leave."

There was an uncomfortable silence. Carolyn's mind raced, and she stared down at her shoes, trying to think clearly. *I have to stay here tonight—I don't have the money to stay on the mainland. . . . I have to stay here and watch the house. . . . Mom's counting on me to take over—*

"Can you stay and eat?" Carolyn asked Andy, then felt her heart sink as he shook his head.

"I'd like to, but I can't. I've got that tour tonight."

He didn't look very happy about it. As Carolyn got out of the car and gazed back at him, she decided he looked about as upset as she was feeling.

Joss pulled back from Andy's door. He was standing in deep shadows where Carolyn couldn't see his face.

"Too bad," Joss said softly. "Maybe some other time."

"Count on it," Andy replied.

He looked as if he was going to say more, but Joss never gave him the chance. In one fluid movement Joss was at Carolyn's side, taking her elbow and guiding her to the porch. Nora was standing there holding the door, and as Carolyn started in, she suddenly remembered something and ran back to the steps, waving her arms at the car.

"Andy, wait!"

She saw him slam on the brakes, saw him stretch his head out the window.

"Yeah?" he called.

"Do you know anything about a key?"

"What? I can't hear you!"

"A key!" Carolyn yelled. "I found *this key*—"

"No, it's not risky!" Andy yelled back. "I take the boat out at night all the time! See you tomorrow!"

"No, Andy—wait!"

But the taillights of Andy's car faded and disappeared.

And when Carolyn turned around, both Nora and Joss were standing beside the front door, waiting for her.

13

CAROLYN SAT AT THE KITCHEN TABLE, WATCHING JOSS slice the meatloaf. Nora had gone, leaving them alone, and she thought wistfully of Andy. Joss rinsed his hands at the sink, then slid them over the back of his jeans to dry them off. He wasn't wearing the vest now—instead he had on a cable-knit sweater that was an offwhite color and several sizes too big.

"I see you got some clothes," she said as he put the platter in front of her on the table.

"Nora found it for me." He glanced up, and she felt the deep dark pull of his eyes. "I'm glad your mother's all right." He sat down across from her and moved his chair closer. "With a fall like that . . . well. You never know."

"How'd it happen?" Carolyn asked bluntly.

His eyes were calm upon her face.

"I don't know."

"You weren't with her?" Carolyn persisted. "You didn't see her fall?"

"She'd gone upstairs to do some cleaning, and I was outside. When I came in, I called her, but she didn't answer. I started looking for her, and that's when I noticed some broken glass lying out in the hall. She must have lost her balance somehow and tipped the ladder over. It fell onto the dresser and broke the mirror—I guess that's how she hit her head and cut herself so bad."

Carolyn cringed at his recollection. "Where was Nora all that time?"

"I don't know."

He watched her a moment, then shook his head.

"I'm sorry. If I'd been with her, maybe it wouldn't have happened."

Carolyn nodded slowly. She wanted to blame him —wanted to blame Nora—wanted most of all to blame herself. But instead she looked into his eyes and said, "You called for help. With everything going on around here, I never thanked you for that."

"I just want her to get well."

"The thing *she* wants most right now is to get this place in shape." Carolyn sighed. "I know her. And once she starts feeling better, she'll be lying in the hospital thinking more about this stupid house than her own condition."

She clenched her fists and held them tight against her forehead, trying to push back the headache pounding there.

"She was so excited about coming to the island— and I wasn't. She didn't have doubts about this place, but I did. This sure doesn't help my attitude any."

He smiled then. His eyes, for a brief instant, seemed almost warm.

"Maybe having this accident will convince her to go back."

"Mom? Are you kidding?" Carolyn sighed.

"Nora told me most people around here don't think the house is worth saving. Not worth putting a lot of time and money into—"

"And you agree with them, I suppose?" Carolyn almost snapped at him.

"I didn't say that."

She closed her eyes and took a deep breath. "People don't understand my mom. When she has her heart set on something, there's no changing her mind. It'd take more than a fall to do that."

He didn't answer right away. He pushed his fork slowly into his meat. He stared at it and said without looking up, "Your mother's a very strong woman."

"Yes, she is." Despite Carolyn's anger, a feeling of pride crept in, lessening the pain in her heart.

"You're very close."

Carolyn nodded. "Especially since Dad died. We've had to lean on each other a lot."

"She loves you very much, I know," Joss went on quietly. For an instant his eyes lifted to her face. "If anything happened to you, she'd be devastated."

Carolyn nodded, more to herself than to him. "I feel the same way about her."

She stabbed at her potato, then put her fork down on her plate. Nothing looked good to her. She had no desire at all to eat.

"She said your name at the hospital," Carolyn said, and Joss hesitated, his fork in midair.

"Did she?" he asked softly, and Carolyn nodded.

"She mentioned you and then she mentioned the

paper and she also said 'house.'" When he didn't respond, she gave a short laugh. "See, what'd I tell you? Even unconscious, she's still worrying about fixing this place up and getting it advertised."

Silence fell between them. The house shuddered in the night wind, and even the quiet was filled with the sound of the sea.

"Tell me about the ghosts," Joss said.

Carolyn glanced at him, startled. She saw him push his plate aside. He crossed his arms on the table and waited.

"Sorry?" Carolyn tried to sound casual, though her heart had taken a dive into her stomach. She put her glass down and smiled politely as though she hadn't heard.

"The ghosts," Joss said again.

His long fingers drummed quietly against his sleeves. Carolyn noticed a cut on the back of one hand and the jagged line of dried blood.

"—in him?" Joss asked.

Carolyn jumped, her face flushing. "I—what?"

Joss's dark glance slid down to his hands, hesitated, then shifted back again to her face.

"Broken glass," he said, a hint of amusement in his voice.

Carolyn blushed again and looked away.

"And what I asked was," Joss repeated, "do you believe in them?"

"What—what ghosts are you talking about?" she stammered.

"Don't you know?"

His eyes settled calmly on her face, and though Carolyn still wasn't looking at him, she could *feel* those eyes—their power, their intensity—forcing her attention back again. Helplessly she returned his gaze. Her heart raced, and her mouth felt dry. She knew she couldn't look away now, even if she'd wanted to.

"But you must know," Joss went on. "The ghosts of Glanton House. A captain, right? His wife? Her lover?"

Carolyn felt herself nod. "How . . . how do you know about that?"

"Nora," he said simply. "She seems convinced the captain's hanging around. Or visiting from time to time, at any rate."

"Then you believe in ghosts?"

"They have as much right here as we do. More, in fact."

It wasn't the answer she'd expected—especially from him—and her eyes widened in surprise.

"What did Nora tell you about the captain?" she asked.

"She told me why he built the house and about his murder. She told me about Carolyn."

Carolyn gave a wry smile. "Some coincidence, huh?"

"Your mother thinks you're taking all this too seriously," Joss said. "She thinks you're scaring yourself."

"She thinks I'm seeing and hearing things that aren't really there." Carolyn was annoyed. "Just like Hazel did before she died. Don't you see the pattern?"

When Joss didn't answer, she leaned forward, her voice lowering urgently.

"The captain's wife and I have the same name. *I'm* seeing ghosts and Hazel saw ghosts. Both Hazel *and* Carolyn Glanton died—so am I wrong to feel a little paranoid?"

For a few minutes Joss stared at her. Then he reached across the table, his hand closing lightly over hers.

"Believing makes you vulnerable. Believing opens the door to strange and powerful things."

For a minute Carolyn stared deep into his eyes, and then slowly she pulled back, sliding her hand free.

"So," she said tightly, "what you're saying is that you agree with my mother."

"That's not at all what I said."

"That you think I'm making everything up—that you think I'm crazy—"

"What I'm saying," Joss said firmly, "is that the more you believe in something, the more control it has over you. Control that could be dangerous."

"You're not making any sense." She stiffened back in her chair and glared at him. "You're patronizing me just like everyone else does, and to tell you the truth, I think your philosophy is really stupid."

She got up from the table and rinsed her plate at the sink. She wiped her hands on the dish towel, then finally she turned back to face him.

"And another thing—"

She broke off and stared at Joss's empty chair.

Her glance went quickly around the room, but the kitchen was deserted.

"Joss?" Carolyn whispered.

She heard the sea crashing and the wailing of the wind.

She put her hands over her ears, but she couldn't shut them out.

Just like she couldn't ignore the house shivering around her . . . as though it feared some new tragedy yet to come.

14

THAT NIGHT CAROLYN LOCKED HER DOOR.

For a long time she stood against it, listening, not even sure what she was listening for.

The house lay huge and silent and secretive around her. She had just decided to turn in when suddenly she heard Joss's door creaking. A second later muffled footsteps moved slowly past her room, and something rattled at the end of the hall.

The locked door?

Is he trying to get into the attic?

The noises stopped, and Carolyn strained her ears through the silence. Part of her wanted to go out there and investigate—the other part couldn't even bring herself to open the bedroom door. *What's he doing?* To her growing uneasiness, she heard him retracing his steps, only this time it sounded as if he were pausing outside every bedroom along the way . . . going inside of it . . . coming back out again.

Like he's looking for something . . . but what?

She heard him go downstairs.

Holding her breath, Carolyn inched open her bedroom door and tried to listen as Joss made his way through the rooms below. Faint tapping sounds drifted up to her, and she could swear that things were being moved from time to time. At last his footsteps faded in the direction of the kitchen, and the cellar door opened and shut. And then the sounds stopped.

Feeling guilty, Carolyn pulled her door closed and berated herself for eavesdropping. *He's probably just working on something down there that needs fixing. He's probably just going over every inch of this old place like Mom asked him to, seeing what needs to be done.*

She wasn't sure how long she stood there. As time dragged on and he didn't come back, Carolyn finally gave up and got ready for bed.

She threw her jeans over the back of a chair, and the key fell out of her pocket, bouncing off the edge of the rug and onto the wooden floor. Carolyn picked it up and groaned softly. She'd wanted so much to ask Andy about it, but he hadn't understood what she was trying to tell him. Slowly she placed it on her nightstand and made herself a mental note. *Talk to him about it tomorrow.*

Her head swam with too many thoughts . . . too many unanswered questions. Faces and events ran together in a blur—*Joss's arrival . . . the trip to the village . . . Molly McClure . . . Mom's accident . . . the trip home from the hospital with Andy . . . Joss's comments in the kitchen . . .*

That key . . .

Carolyn propped herself up in bed and stared at the

key on her bedside table. If not a door key, then what? It was so small, it certainly didn't look important . . . and yet something about it intrigued her.

Had someone put it there on purpose and then lost it? Hazel maybe? According to Andy, Hazel's behavior had been getting stranger and stranger toward the end of her life—had she been losing things, too? Hiding things? Or had someone from some other time, some other century maybe, put the key there for safekeeping and never come back to retrieve it?

There you go again . . . you and your imagination . . .

Carolyn turned restlessly on her pillow. Like a fast-forwarded movie, her mind went through the house, trying to picture every possible place for a key. Doors were out—but furniture? Armoires and bureaus and trunks? Frustrated, she shook her head and tried to think. No . . . she'd already looked through the furniture searching for Hazel's clothes. And not only had everything been unlocked, most had been empty.

Carolyn picked the key up again and turned it over in her hand. She started to put it in the drawer of her nightstand, then, on an impulse, slipped it onto the chain around her neck.

She lay in bed, eyes wide, staring at the ceiling. *I'm not going to scare myself. I'm going to sleep tonight just like I did last night. I'm perfectly all right, and nothing's going to happen.*

For a long time, nothing did.

The wind buffeted the old house, whistling into cracks and corners, creaking the foundations and whining beneath the eaves. The sea swelled and broke upon the rocks, its angry thunder filling the night—her bedroom—her pounding head—and as something rattled against the windowpanes, Carolyn realized that it really *was* thundering outside—*storming* in fact—and she dived beneath her blankets.

The rushing and roaring continued till she thought she'd scream. In desperation she groped for the lamp and turned it on, relieved when the room flooded with soft light. *If I could just find some aspirin, maybe then I could sleep. . . .*

Flinging off the covers, she padded to her door and looked out, squinting into the gloom. Across the hall, Joss's door was shut, no sound from the other side. *He must be sleeping. . . . I wonder when he came back?* She couldn't remember where the light switch was, so she began feeling along the wall.

Moving as quietly as she could, Carolyn made her way down the corridor, with only the faint light from her bedroom to guide her. As she neared the end of the hall, she could see the attic door ahead of her, dark and foreboding, and she forced herself to stop and touch the doorknob.

Locked.

Just like Nora said.

I didn't imagine it—I couldn't have—and yet I must have—everything must have been a dream. . . .

Carolyn stared at the doorknob, her heart lodged in her throat. Again the images flashed through her mind—the stains on the walls and floor—the scraping and clawing . . . the runny pool around her feet. . . . *"And then he stole into Glanton House one dark, dark night and ripped Carolyn and her lover to bits. . . ."*

She hurried to the bathroom. She slammed the door and leaned against it, drawing slow, unsteady breaths. She felt hot again and sick to her stomach. *Nightmare —just a nightmare—but I won't have it again tonight —I'll find that aspirin and sleep like a baby—*

She rummaged through the medicine cabinet, but didn't find anything she could use. She splashed cold water over her face again and again. All that gossip and theorizing from Nora and Andy and Molly and Joss—well, she'd certainly learned her lesson, all right. In the future, she wouldn't ask anyone anything, and she wouldn't *believe* anything, either.

"Oh, Mom," Carolyn whispered, "I wish you were home."

The bathroom quivered as thunder burst close to the house. Quickly Carolyn let herself out into the hall again.

She'd gotten halfway to her room when there was an eerie hum, and the light in her doorway disappeared.

Carolyn froze, every muscle locked. Her ears strained through the brief silence, but then the wind and sea and storm rushed in, surging through the house as though the very walls were invisible and helpless to stop them.

The lights have gone out again—that's all—that's all it is—just keep going the way you were going— your room's right there—just at the end of the hall—go on—you can do it—

But she *couldn't* do it, not at first. The hall was so black that she couldn't see her hand in front of her face. Groping blindly, she found the wall behind her and backed against it, waiting for her eyes to adjust to the gloom.

And then she heard it.

So slow . . . so faint beneath the storm, that at first she couldn't be sure it was even real. . . .

But then she *knew* it was real—the creaking sound —she could hear it going on and on and on—slow and stealthy and agonizing—echoing through the blackness—a door opening very carefully . . . very purposefully—as though someone didn't want to be heard. . . .

The attic . . .

It *was* the attic—*wasn't it?*

In her terrible fear Carolyn couldn't tell *where* the sound was coming from—ahead of her, behind her, or only in her mind. She gripped the wall with clawed fingers and held her breath, and the creaking went on . . . on . . . then ended abruptly, swallowed by the rage of the storm.

It came to her then that maybe it wasn't the attic at all—maybe it was Joss. Joss coming out to find the bathroom maybe, or to go back downstairs. Joss wakened and restless from the storm, Joss trying to turn the lights back on, Joss wandering around in the dark as helpless as she—

"Joss!" she called.

No answer.

Against her back, the wall trembled like paper beneath the onslaught of the wind. Once more Carolyn inched her way through the pitch blackness, trying to find her room.

The crash was loud and terrible.

As a gust of wind swept through the hallway, Carolyn screamed and hid her face against the wall.

"Joss! Joss, is that you?"

But the crashing came again—and again—loud and terrifying and relentless, and the hall was cold and filled with wind, and somewhere in the back of Carolyn's mind, a crazy thought began to form that maybe—somehow—the attic door was open, banging back and forth against the wall.

"Joss!" she shouted. *Why can't he hear me—how can anyone sleep through this racket, but right now I have to stop that noise—that awful noise—have to latch the door before I go out of my mind—*

Carolyn didn't need a flashlight now—she just followed the icy trail of the wind. *Yes, yes, the attic door—it must be the attic door—somehow the storm's blown in from the widow's walk and gusted down the stairs and opened this door, too—broken the lock after all this time—because the lock is so old and the door is so old and it wouldn't take much to break it—*

But that other thought was in her head, too, nagging at her as she tried to find the door in the darkness—*screaming* at her even though she tried to make it stop—*and maybe it wasn't a dream after all, Carolyn—maybe the attic door was really open that night because ghosts don't worry about locks, do they? Locks and walls and doors mean nothing to ghosts, they can do whatever they want—to whoever they want—*

"Joss!" Carolyn screamed again.

But she'd found the door at last, found the cold, cold night whipping down the stairs. *I've got to go up there—I've got to go up and fasten that other door. . . .*

She squinted into the darkness at the top of the stairs. She stood for a long time, trying to get up the courage to just move, and suddenly she thought she saw a light high above her—just a tiny pinpoint of light that flickered for a second, then disappeared.

A candle? No, in all that wind, it was impossible. . . .

A flashlight?

"Joss?" Carolyn called. "Is that you?"

And then it came again.

A tiny, brief flickering . . . so quick that it was gone again almost before she even saw it.

Swallowing a cry, Carolyn lifted the hem of her long nightgown and started slowly up the stairs.

15

IT SEEMED TO TAKE FOREVER.

As Carolyn put one foot ahead of the other, she could feel her muscles cramping, could feel low sobs of fear in her throat. She wanted to run, to turn around and leave this house and never come back. She thought of her mother lying still and white in the hospital bed, of her mother's hopes for this strange old house—she thought of her own promise to stay and make it work—

"I can do this," Carolyn muttered to herself. Back home if she'd heard strange noises in the night, she'd always been able to talk herself out of being scared. *But this isn't home . . . this will never be home—*

She stopped. She stood on the stairs and got a firm grip on herself and tried to blank the fear out of her mind. She tried to tell herself that it was just a normal old storm and a normal old door in a normal old attic, and that all she had to do was *close* that stupid old door and go back to bed. *Simple as that, Carolyn. Piece of cake.*

She felt half frozen. She was shivering all over. Not just from the cold. From fear.

"Go on," she muttered again. "Go on!"

She couldn't see the light anymore. She must have imagined that, too, just like she'd imagined being up here that other night—just like she'd imagined the creaking sound in the hall just before the attic door had blown open. . . .

"But I'm not imagining this," she told herself fiercely. *This is real.*

She'd reached the top at last. She kept one hand on the banister to steady herself, and she looked slowly around the attic, her eyes wide.

The door to the widow's walk was wide open. It had blown back against the wall and rain was lashing in, sweeping in sheets across the floor. There was no moon, and yet somehow she could *see*—could sense her way across the floor, to that other threshold that led out to the walkway beyond.

Carolyn walked over to the door. She stopped and stood in the threshold.

All around her the sky exploded with lightning, and she stared, transfixed.

For just an instant she could see everything.

Everything—the night, the world, the whole universe, it seemed—all from the rooftop of Glanton House.

The panorama was frightening—and yet more beautiful than anything she'd ever witnessed in her whole life.

Black clouds churned across an even blacker sky, boiling high above the house, shot through with jagged bolts of golden fire. The storm raged furiously, clawing and tearing at the night, and beneath its wild shrieking of wind and rain came the frenzied roar of the sea.

Carolyn couldn't move.

Far below her, frantic waves crashed again and again, impaling themselves on razor-sharp rocks, gnashing and gnawing the sheer walls of the cliffs until they bled black foam. The whole world had gone mad.

The sky plunged into total darkness once more. As from a dream, Carolyn roused sluggishly and tried to focus.

And then she saw another light.

It was very distant . . . very surreal, forming slowly through the rain. It hovered there, blurry and wavy, down, down, among the massive rocks at the bottom of the cliffs.

She wanted to look away, but she couldn't.

The light bobbed . . . faded . . . nearly went out.

And then it began to grow—to *throb*—as though there were *life* inside of it, struggling to survive.

"Have you ever seen ghost lights?"

From some remote corner of her mind, she could almost hear Andy's voice again, and she struggled to remember.

"Weird lights glowing down along the water late at night . . . the souls of drowned sailors . . . can't rest till they're reunited with what they loved most in life."

The light went out.

Startled, Carolyn stood there holding on to the

doorframe, bracing herself against the rain. Her night-gown was soaking wet; her hair blew wildly around her face, and she put up a hand to brush it from her eyes.

Yes . . . yes . . . there it is—the light again!

Her heart quickened in excitement and fear. Slowly she moved out onto the widow's walk, oblivious to the groaning of boards beneath her bare feet.

And she could see it now—hovering in midair—fuzzy and indistinct through the storm—and it seemed to be moving—drifting into the rocks, drifting out again—but maybe it was only the rain distorting it, only the wind blowing it, she couldn't tell. She only knew it was there and that it seemed to be struggling with the storm, and that suddenly—*somehow*—she wanted to help it, just as that other Carolyn must have wanted to help those poor doomed sailors that night of the storm—

And maybe it is one of those sailors—maybe it's one of those sailors struggling and dying down there—struggling all for nothing, because he's doomed to drown over and over and over again until he's finally reunited with the one he loved most in life—

"*Maaathewww!*"

Carolyn's heart gave a jolt.

She looked around wildly, trying to see, and then to her horror the sound came again.

"*Maaathewww!*"

It came out from nowhere, and yet she'd heard it before—she *knew* she'd heard it before—when she'd been exploring along the cliffs—a voice blown away on the wind, striking a chord deep, deep in her soul—

"Maaathewww!"

She stepped farther out onto the walkway, her hands in her hair now, trying to keep it from her eyes, trying to peer into the darkness where that strange hazy light bobbed and dipped among the deathrocks near the water—

"Is anyone there!" Carolyn screamed. "Where are you?"

And in her mind she saw the battered ship—the bodies tossed about helplessly by the waves—the captain's face contorted in shock as he watched his hand being chopped off and he realized he was going to die—*but you know it's not really happening now, don't you, Carolyn—you know you're just dreaming— just imagining things—you don't really hear Captain Glanton calling his own name—it's just the shriek and howl of the wind—*

"Where are you!" she screamed again. "Is anyone there?"

And she was sobbing now, because the call sounded so desperate, so pleading, and she felt its pain, its loneliness, as deep and as real as her own pain and loneliness—

"Maathewww . . ." the voice mocked her, and Carolyn screamed back at it—

"Stop it! You're not real! You're only in my mind!"

She was as far as she could go now, standing on the widow's walk, her hands around the railing, and she could feel the soggy weight of her nightgown whipping around her, and her hair streaming wildly in the wind, and she leaned forward, straining far, far over the endless abyss of the night—

She didn't hear the boards giving out beneath her.

Didn't hear the sudden groan and snap of old wood rotting through, the rusty creak of the railing swinging away . . .

And in that last coherent second, Carolyn only felt a strange, slow surprise as the darkness rushed up to meet her.

16

"CAROLYN!"

She could hear it, somewhere through the wind, a voice calling her, but a different voice this time, not the one by the cliffs, not the one from the storm—

"Carolyn! Hang on!"

Reality slammed into her with such force that she reeled from the impact. As she screamed and screamed again, she realized she was dangling in midair, wind and rain lashing her from all sides, and that someone high above was holding on to one of her hands.

"Help!" Carolyn shrieked. "Oh, God, help me!"

"Hold on!" the voice shouted again. "Whatever you do, don't let go! You hear me, Carolyn? You hold on!"

"I can't! I'm slipping!"

"No, you're not—I've got you! Don't look down!"

But she did look down—before she could stop herself, she looked down and saw the stormy blackness around her, the sheer drop beneath her, and as she swung helplessly in the air, lightning ripped from the churning clouds, suspending everything in an eerie glow.

"I'm falling!" she sobbed, and there were strong hands around her wrist, and she was flopping through the air like a rag doll as someone began pulling her up.

"You're not falling! Give me your other hand— reach up and hold on to me! Do it, Carolyn—do it *now!*"

With a superhuman effort, she managed to twist her body and fling her other arm upward, crying out in terror as it swept uselessly through empty air and threw her off balance.

"Try it again, Carolyn! Reach for me!"

She was practically hysterical now, but somehow she did it. This time her hand met with something solid, and seconds later she felt herself being drawn up with agonizing slowness. The wind tossed her like a sail—her arms felt wrenched from their sockets. After an eternity, she felt the jagged edge of the balcony and then arms were around her, pulling her the rest of the way to safety. With one last cry she fell through the doorway and onto the attic floor.

For a long time she lay there, shivering and disoriented.

The attic was unnaturally quiet after the deafening roar of the storm.

And when she finally tried to sit up, she realized that someone was holding her—that she was pressed against his bare chest, with his heartbeat strong and steady beneath her cheek. . . .

"Carolyn," Joss murmured, "it's okay . . . you're safe."

Slowly she raised her eyes, gazing into the half shadow of his face. She could smell night and wind and rain on his skin, in his hair, and as his arms tightened around her, she choked back a sob.

"Don't," Joss said quietly. "Everything's all right."

"But—but—" She couldn't even talk, her voice was shaking so badly, like her body was shaking and her teeth were chattering, and her heart was pounding out of control—"I went out there—I thought I heard—"

"Carolyn," he whispered. He put one hand to her forehead and gently smoothed back her hair. He was so close to her now, only the clinging fabric of her nightgown separated them. In the darkness she felt the slight shift of his body, and then his lips were on hers, his fingers stroking her cheeks, his kiss long and deep and tender.

Carolyn felt his hands slide down her neck, onto her shoulders. She shivered as they moved slowly down her arms, wrapping around her waist, pressing her even closer.

She tilted her face up to his. She slipped her arms around his neck and clung to him. His lips moved to her throat and lingered there, and as she drew her breath in sharply, he suddenly released her and pulled away.

"Go downstairs," he said, and his voice sounded hoarse and strained, hollow in the darkness of the room. "Get into something dry. Then we'll talk."

"No—you don't understand—"

"Come on." He was forcing her to her feet now, shining a flashlight ahead of them, leading her back down the stairs and along the second-floor hallway.

"Go in and change. Then you can tell me what happened."

Even in her current state, Carolyn sensed somehow that he was angry with her. *Because of the accident? Because of the kiss? Going out there was a stupid thing to do—I could have killed myself and him, too—*

"Hurry up," Joss said tightly. "I'll be in the kitchen."

He is mad. Well, can I blame him?

"I'm so sorry," she mumbled, "it's just that I saw that light—heard that voice—" but Joss's grip was almost painful, and he cut her off with a shake of his head.

"Change your clothes," he ordered.

She was too drained to argue. She closed her door and fell across her bed, burying her face in the pillow. *What happened up there in the attic?* Her mind raced, and her heart beat frantically. Something horrible, *but he rescued me. . . .* Something deadly, *but he saved my life.*

She'd never been kissed like that before. In the safety of her room, Carolyn closed her eyes and tried to shut out everything that had happened up there, but she could still feel it—Joss's kiss—his lips on hers, insistent, demanding—and how she'd responded with a startling intensity of her own.

What's he going to think of me?

She couldn't face him. There was no way she could get dressed and go downstairs now and sit there calmly discussing her accident and look him in the eye without reliving that kiss.

But she had to go, of course. Sooner or later she'd

have to face him again . . . *so it might as well be tonight.*

Without warning the lights blinked on—dimmed —then brightened back to full power. Carolyn stared at her bedside lamp, then out at the flashes of lightning beyond her window. *Maybe he thought I was hysterical and I wasn't responsible for my actions and I won't remember what happened, and maybe if I'm really lucky he'll forget about the whole thing.*

But she thought of his kiss again, and how she'd felt wrapped tightly within the strength of his arms, and her whole body went so hot and weak, she could hardly change clothes.

Joss was at the stove when she finally got to the kitchen. His feet were bare, and his wet jeans clung to him like a second skin. Still shirtless, he'd draped a towel around his neck and smoothed his damp hair back behind his ears. The kitchen smelled warm and homey, and Carolyn saw that he was making cocoa. At first he didn't seem to realize she was even there, so she had time to slip into a chair and compose herself before he glanced over and nodded.

"Thought you could use something hot to drink," he said softly.

She swallowed and forced a smile. "Thanks. That's nice."

He kept standing there stirring the spoon in the pan. Caroline kneaded her fingers together, rested her hands on the tabletop, and stared at them.

"You could have been killed tonight," Joss said at last. "I guess you know that."

"I do know that." Carolyn's voice got slightly

defensive. "I really don't know what to say. You saved my life. I can't think of anything grateful enough to—"

"Forget it," Joss said.

"Forget it? But if you hadn't been there—"

"It's okay." He lifted his hand in a gesture for silence. Carolyn twisted her fingers together until they ached.

"Joss—"

"I guess you had a good *reason* for going out there."

He sounded ready for anything, no matter how stupid her reason might turn out to be, so Carolyn took a deep breath and plunged in. She told him about the power going out, and how the attic door had been open; how she'd heard the voice calling and seen the distant light only seconds before her accident. She told him everything, and during the whole time he just kept stirring the pan and not talking, until finally she couldn't stand it any longer.

"Well, aren't you going to say something?" she demanded.

He turned around and fixed her with a calm, dark stare.

"What do you want me to say?"

"Well . . . that you believe me would certainly be a good start."

He seemed to be considering this. He turned back to the stove.

"I'm not making it up!" Carolyn insisted. "I didn't imagine it! And I've heard that voice before when I was out on the cliffs! I almost fell that time, too!"

He shot her a quick look she couldn't read. He put the spoon down and filled two mugs with cocoa.

"The boards on the widow's walk were rotted through," he said quietly. "The railing wasn't even attached to the platform."

"Do you think I would have gone out there if I'd known that?" Carolyn looked down as he put the mug in front of her. "I saw a *light*, Joss. At the bottom of the cliffs. It was *real.*"

He paused beside her chair. She glanced up at him, feeling somehow that she had to defend herself.

"It wasn't very clear at first, but then it grew stronger—or at least it *seemed* as if it was trying to grow stronger. It was moving along the rocks, but it was hard to see because of all the rain."

He mumbled something she couldn't hear. He stared at the wall above her head.

"What did you say?" Carolyn asked.

"I said . . . ghost lights."

Joss moved slowly to the window. Carolyn watched as he parted the curtains and stared out into the night.

"Help from the living," he murmured. "Yes . . . of course . . ."

Carolyn was feeling sicker by the minute. "But ghost lights are just make-believe! Silly superstitions—"

"That depends," Joss said, "on who sees them."

"But I *did* see them! Whatever they were—they were *real!*"

Joss shook his head and let the curtains fall back into place.

"Well, of course you can't see them from here, if that's what you're looking for!" Carolyn's voice rose thinly, and she stood up from her chair. "You can't see them from here—you have to be up high! You're just trying to scare me! You're just trying to make me think I imagined everything!"

Joss's glance slid smoothly back over his shoulder . . . settled onto her face. "I don't know what you mean."

"Where were you when I first called?" Tears sprang to Carolyn's eyes, and she fiercely blinked them back. "When that door blew open, and it sounded like a hurricane in the hall?"

"Asleep. The wind blows strongest at my corner of the house—it's hard to hear anything—*especially* when you're asleep."

"Then how did you finally hear me in time? Just in time to keep me from falling? And how did you know where I was—and how did you get there so fast and—"

"Stop it, Carolyn," Joss said. He had ahold of her shoulders now, shaking her gently. "You've been through a lot tonight; you need some rest. Things will look a lot different in the morning—"

"No!"

She wrenched from his grasp, but he was still staring at her—his dark, dark eyes pulling her in, holding her, until she couldn't move . . . couldn't even breathe . . .

"Who *are* you?" Carolyn whispered.

Joss said nothing.

He took one step toward her, but Carolyn turned and ran to her room.

17

"IT'S EIGHT IN THE MORNING. WHAT ARE YOU DOING here?"

Carolyn stopped on the front porch and frowned at the figure lounging there on the steps at her feet.

"Hi." Andy grinned. "How's it going?"

"Terrible, if you must know," Carolyn muttered, and he jumped up in alarm.

"Is your mom worse? What happened?"

Carolyn glared at him. Joss's words of wisdom still rang in her ears, and as much as she hated to admit it, last night almost *did* seem like a bad dream. The storm had given way to thick wet fog, the wind had calmed to a playful gustiness, and now, instead of lightning and thunder, there was only the rumble and crash of the sea.

She shook her head in wry amusement. So things looked a lot different after all, but that didn't change the fact that she'd fallen from the widow's walk last night—that she'd nearly been killed—*that Joss kissed me*—

"Tell me," Andy insisted, and with a shock, Carolyn realized he was holding both her hands, trying to get her attention.

"No," she mumbled, "no, it's not my mom. I called about an hour ago; she was still sleeping. They say she's going to be okay, but she'll still need to stay there awhile. And they don't really want her to have any visitors yet."

"Sounds good." Andy smiled. When Carolyn didn't return it, he stepped back and fixed her with a quizzical stare. "So what's wrong? You look awful."

"Thanks."

"Come on, Carolyn—I drove all the way out here to see you, and that Joss guy was hammering so loud I had to scream at him, and then he finally answered the door and hardly said two words to me and—" He broke off, eyes narrowing. "Did something happen last night? Are you all right?"

"Yes, something did happen, and yes, I'm all right." Carolyn sighed.

"Wait! Where you going?"

"For a walk. Are you coming with me, or do I have to keep shouting?"

"Whoa!" Andy gave an exaggerated shudder and fell into step beside her. "Someone must have gotten up on the wrong side of bed this morning."

"Sorry," she relented. "It's not your fault I'm in such a rotten mood."

"Well, that's a relief. And since you're obviously not going to tell me what's going on, I might as well tell you why I came out here to see you."

"Are you sure you want to? I might bite your head off."

"I thought we could go into the village and spend the day together. The music competition's this afternoon—and then a food fair tonight. Should be lots of fun."

"I don't feel much like fun. I wouldn't *be* much fun."

"Hey, give me a little credit. Would I have asked you to go if I thought we'd have a terrible time?"

She shook her head, smiling a little. "I shouldn't, you know. I should stay here and work on the house. There's so much to do, I don't even know where to start."

"I thought that's what Joss was here for," Andy reminded her. "And anyway, you'll have plenty of time to get the place in shape. The festival only lasts through the weekend, and you've got the rest of your life to work on the house."

"Oh, Andy"—Carolyn sighed—"the rest of my life was down to about one second last night."

"What? What are you talking about?"

The smile she gave him was strained. "Let's not go into it right now. Not here, anyway."

"Okay," he said slowly, his face puzzled. "Whenever you're ready, I'm all ears."

"Let me get my jacket."

They went back to the house, and Andy waited while Carolyn hunted for her coat. She could hear Joss working on the back porch, and as she went into the kitchen, she found Nora at the sink, polishing a silver tea service.

"Oh, hi, Nora. I didn't hear you come in."

The housekeeper glanced up but said nothing. She rubbed fiercely at the teapot with her rag.

"He told me. What happened last night."

"Who, Joss?" Carolyn was surprised. "You mean about the accident?"

"You *think* it was an accident." Nora's eyes flicked to Carolyn's face, then back again to her work. "Well, it wasn't. You still don't believe. Even after my warning. Well, you deserve it, then. You deserve anything that happens. I can't save you from trouble if you don't want to be saved."

She turned and left the room, leaving Carolyn to stare openmouthed. A second later the back door opened and Joss wandered in. He was studying a ragged-looking piece of paper in his hand, but when he glanced up and saw Carolyn, he quickly stuffed the paper into his hip pocket.

Carolyn stared at him. Was it her imagination or had he looked guilty for one split second? His bulky sweater covered both pocket and paper, and she couldn't see a thing. She raised her eyes and saw him staring back at her.

"How do you feel?" he asked.

The memory of his kiss came back to her, and her cheeks warmed. She saw her jacket on the back of a chair and went over to pick it up, trying to keep her voice casual.

"Okay. I'm going into the village for a while."

Petty things . . . unimportant things . . . when really, what she wanted to say was *Let's talk about what happened last night, let's talk about the accident, about the widow's walk, about the way you held me and why you acted so weird afterward and who you are and*

*where you came from—and what's on that paper you
obviously don't want me to see—*

"I could have let you fall," he said, and it was so
sudden, so totally unexpected, that Carolyn gaped at
him.

"What?"

"If I'd wanted to hurt you," Joss went on matter-of-
factly, "which is what you're wondering right now,
then I would have let you fall. I wouldn't have tried to
save you."

Carolyn was speechless. She saw his lips ease into a
smile, but there was no humor at all in his eyes.
Shaken, she went back to the parlor and told Andy she
was ready to go.

The festival was already gearing up when they got
there. As they wandered through the village, Carolyn
was glad Andy had talked her into coming. Booths
were doing a brisk business, musicians were warming
up on every corner, and the streets were rapidly filling
with people. For several hours they took in the sights,
till Andy finally managed to drag her over to the food
carts.

"I'm starving, Carolyn! I haven't eaten all morning!"

To her surprise, Carolyn realized she hadn't eaten,
either.

"What's your pleasure?" Andy grinned. "My treat."

"Then I'll have one of everything." Carolyn
laughed. "And seconds to go with it."

Andy made a face and quickly scanned the tempt-
ing variety of food vendors.

"There's an unbelievable line at the Mexican booth
right now—but I sure could use some tacos."

At Carolyn's nod, he dashed off through the crowds, leaving her to wait on the corner. She recognized the street as she stood there, and knowing it would take Andy a while to get back, Carolyn walked the last two blocks to the library. Jean was at the front desk and asked about Carolyn's mother, then seemed surprised when Carolyn asked her about the books she'd promised to find.

"I thought you picked them up already," Jean informed her, and this time it was Carolyn's turn to be surprised.

"No," Carolyn said. "I haven't even been in since yesterday."

"I had them here at the desk for you," Jean went on, bewildered. "I had to leave early yesterday, but I'm sure my assistant said she called your house and left a message."

"I never got it," Carolyn told her.

"Well, the books were gone this morning." Jean sighed in exasperation. "Not that I think they've been stolen—but wouldn't you know someone would just come in and take them when they were meant for someone else!"

Jean promised to track them down and get back with her, and after thanking her for all her trouble, Carolyn went back outside. She stood for a minute on the sidewalk, thinking about the books and the message she never got. Then, as she glanced up again, she saw a movement at the front window of the library and recognized Molly McClure.

"Molly!" Carolyn called. She waved and saw Molly lift one hand. She started to yell again and ask Molly to come out and join them for lunch, when suddenly Carolyn sensed someone behind her.

"Hi," a deep voice spoke, and Carolyn whirled around, looking up into Joss's face.

"Joss! What are you doing here?"

At first he didn't answer. Then he gestured toward the intersection at the bottom of the hill.

"I needed some things at the hardware store." His dark eyes narrowed, scanning the crowds. He seemed uneasy. "Where's your friend?"

"Getting something to eat." Carolyn hesitated, then said, "Do you want to have lunch with us?"

"I can't. I have too much to do."

He was making her nervous, and Carolyn glanced anxiously at the food carts. She could see Andy paying at the register, and then she saw his quick double take as he noticed who she was talking to.

"Are you sure?" she asked Joss again. "We could find a table somewhere and sit down."

He shook his head and stepped back. He ran one hand through his hair, and his gaze traveled slowly up the sidewalk, where it suddenly stopped. Carolyn followed the direction of his stare and saw Molly sagging tiredly in the library window.

"I have to go," Joss said abruptly. "I'll see you back at the house."

To Carolyn's dismay, he headed into the crowds. By the time Andy returned, Joss had completely disappeared.

"Hey," Andy said, coming up with three bulging sacks of food. "Where's your friend?"

"He had to go," Carolyn replied uneasily.

"Thought he was too busy to come in today."

"He needed some things at the store," Carolyn said. She bit into the taco Andy gave her, but she was still staring at the crowds. Not a trace of Joss.

"Well," Andy teased, chewing thoughtfully on an enchilada and making a face, "he doesn't know what he's missing. All this good grease."

"He seemed kind of nervous," Carolyn said, missing the joke.

"Yeah? Wonder why?"

Carolyn shook her head and reached for Andy's arm.

"Can we find someplace to sit down? I want to tell you what happened last night."

She waved again to Molly as they passed the library, and felt Andy nudge her as he pointed to a spot up the street.

"Look—there's a bench. Grab it!"

They hurried over before anyone else came along, then sat down and spread out their picnic between them.

Carolyn stared at Andy and sighed.

"I don't know why I'm telling you this. I don't even know what's going on. It sounds stupid when I try to put it into words."

Andy groaned. "I knew it. Joss asked you to run away with him, and you're going."

"What?" Carolyn pulled back in surprise. "No!"

"Hmmm," Andy mused, studying her face. "But you *blushed* just now, so something tells me I'm not going to hear *every* detail about what happened last night."

Carolyn pointedly ignored him. "I fell off the widow's walk. In the middle of the storm."

"*What!*" Now it was Andy's turn to look surprised. "What—are you *crazy*, Carolyn? What were you doing up there in the first place—don't you know that thing's falling apart?"

"I know, I know, you don't have to remind me. Just be quiet, and let me finish."

Andy settled back on the bench and crossed his arms over his chest, nodding at her to go on. Carolyn told the story as simply and factually as she could— the attic door—the voice—the light—her fall—her rescue. She left out the part about Joss's kiss.

"As much as I hate to say it"—Andy sighed—"I guess it was a good thing Joss was there."

Carolyn didn't answer.

Andy looked down at their lunch. Now that Carolyn had finished her story, they'd both lost their appetites.

"Where's this guy from?" Andy finally asked.

"I don't know. He's just a drifter. I don't know anything about him. Except that he's . . . I don't know. Strange."

They were silent for a moment. Then Andy said softly, "You're afraid of him, aren't you."

Carolyn hesitated . . . nodded.

"You don't know anything about him," Andy went on carefully.

"No."

"Except that he saved your life."

"He might have saved my life, but he still gives me the creeps."

"Then tell him to leave," Andy said reasonably.

"I'm not real keen on the idea of him being in the house alone with you anyway."

"Well . . . Mom seemed to think he was okay—she *wanted* him to stay."

"Yeah, well, don't forget what happened to the captain's wife when she let *her* drifter stay."

At Carolyn's startled expression, Andy reached over and gave her a playful hug.

"I'm kidding! It's a joke! Look"—he sighed—"I just want you to be careful, that's all. Your mom's gonna see the positive side of *anything* if it means she can get that house ready for business." He wiped his mouth with his napkin. "I'm sorry, it's none of my business and I shouldn't be so critical—I don't know the guy, either, but if you feel that uncomfortable about him, then you should tell him to leave."

"I can't just tell him that."

"Sure you can. You look at him, and you smile, and you say, 'Joss, leave.' "

"It's not that simple, Andy. We really need Joss there. We need him to finish the house."

"Nothing's worth that, and you know it. Nothing's worth being afraid—*especially* in your own house."

"Well, I can't do it," Carolyn said miserably. "Not after he saved Mom's life and mine, too."

She stared down at her uneaten food. Then she wadded everything up in the greasy paper and angrily stuffed it into the litter can behind their bench.

"Come on, Carolyn, you've got to eat," Andy coaxed, but she shook her head and stood up. "Great" —Andy sighed—"now you're mad."

"No, I'm not."

"Yes, you are."

Carolyn shook her head adamantly. "No, I'm not. And if I am, it's only at myself. Sometimes I think I'm losing my mind, Andy—I don't know what to think about anything, and I'm suspicious of *everything!* I'm not even sure the things I heard last night were real. Or the things I saw that first night, either. Sometimes I can't tell anymore if I'm awake or asleep. I mean, maybe *you're* not real—maybe I'm dreaming you right now."

She took off up the hill and heard him running after her.

"Carolyn, wait up. Hey, don't be like that."

"Be like what? Confused? Scared? This whole thing is so stupid and mixed up, I can't stand it."

She kicked angrily at a rock and watched it bounce against a nearby building. Several passersby turned to stare at her, and after a brief moment of indecision, Andy put his arm around her shoulders.

"Look, Carolyn, have I brought this up before? Grief—moving—worry—mom in hospital—you've been under a *ton* of stress. Not to mention the fact that your house is falling down around your ears, *and* you inherited a housekeeper who's the spitting image of your worst nightmare."

Carolyn kept walking but managed a smile at the last remark.

"So give yourself permission to feel a little vulnerable right now. A little mixed-up. A little bit paranoid."

Believing makes you vulnerable. . . .

Carolyn stopped, frowning. Andy gave her a gentle shake and leaned in close to her face.

"Hey . . . you fading out on me? What's wrong?"

"Nothing. I mean . . . just something Joss said once."

"Joss again." Andy groaned. "Now *I'm* getting paranoid."

He stopped walking and pulled her back to face him. His blue eyes crinkled up, and his irresistible grin slowly widened. He pulled her close in a bear hug and planted a firm kiss on her cheek.

"Come on. Let's have some fun, what do you say?"

His arms were warm and strong. *Don't think about Joss.* . . . Pressed against him, Carolyn felt wonderfully and incredibly safe. *I refuse to think about Joss.* . . . She shifted just enough to peer into Andy's face, and then she smiled.

"Thanks," she murmured.

"Don't thank me."

"No, I really mean it."

"I know you do, but don't thank me anyway."

He laughed and let her go, grabbing her hand and dragging her up the street.

"Where are we going?" Carolyn asked, trying to keep up as the incline grew steeper.

"You wanted to know about the history of your house, didn't you?" Andy teased.

"Yes, but what's up here?"

"The churchyard."

"What?"

"You heard me. The churchyard. Where Carolyn Glanton is buried."

"Do I really want to see this?" Carolyn asked uncertainly.

"Sure you do. It's the prettiest place in the whole village."

Carolyn had her doubts, but when they finally reached the top of the hill, she had to admit Andy was right. The little church was set far back from the road on a secluded side street, its weathered stone walls surrounded by thick green foliage, its steeple rising and disappearing into a leafy canopy of trees. Surprisingly, there were no tourists up this way. The air was very still, and birds sang softly overhead. As Andy led the way around the building, Carolyn saw the low stone wall enclosing the side yard of the church, and the uneven rows of crumbling headstones resting quietly in the cool shadows.

"It's beautiful," she breathed, and Andy nodded, smiling.

"Didn't I tell you? It's the oldest building on the island, and probably the most peaceful spot."

"Do people still get buried here?"

He shook his head and held out his hand to her, leading her deeper and deeper through the graves.

"These are also the oldest *residents* of the island. There's a new cemetery over on the mainland where all the locals have to be buried now. This one's full."

Carolyn could hardly speak, she was so overcome with its beauty. She followed Andy silently, weaving in and out between the ancient markers, and when they finally neared the back of the yard, he let go of her hand and hurried ahead.

"It's right over here!" he hissed back over her shoulder. "It's one of the prettiest graves in the whole place. Legend says that for years and years someone left flowers at her grave on the eve of Carolyn's death—and no one ever found out who it was."

Carolyn shivered. The story was romantic but also unnerving. She'd had enough of ghostly things to last a lifetime; she wanted to stay in the real world for a while.

"Andy," she called softly, "I don't think I want to see it. Let's go back."

She waited for him to answer, but there was only silence.

"Andy?" she tried again. "Are you trying to scare me?"

Carolyn stopped in her tracks and slowly wrapped her arms around herself, her voice going thin and tight.

"Andy, stop it. You just said I'm stressed out, so why are you playing this stupid game with—"

He burst through the shrubbery so unexpectedly that she screamed and jumped away.

"Andy! What are you trying to . . . Andy?"

Alarmed, she stared into his too-white face. He was gesturing behind him, but no sound was coming from his open mouth.

"Andy?" Carolyn's voice shook. "What is it?"

All he could do was point. Spurred by some morbid curiosity, Carolyn pushed past him and swept the low-hanging branches aside, only to stop again a few yards farther with a strange feeling in the pit of her stomach.

She saw the marker on the ground before her . . .

saw the inscription, dark and stained, yet still readable after all these many years . . .

BELOVED CAROLYN

But it wasn't the inscription that held her there, that froze the scream rising fast in her throat—

It was the grave.

The grave below Carolyn Glanton's headstone . . .

The long, muddy hole that yawned black . . . and deep . . . and empty.

18

"WELL . . ." ANDY SIGHED, PAUSING ON THE SIDEWALK outside the sheriff's office. "You've got to admit, when I promise a girl a good time, I always supply plenty of excitement."

Carolyn threw him a look, and he grinned sheepishly.

"Okay, okay, not funny. And I know what you're thinking, and you're right. There are better ways to spend a weekend than being interrogated like two criminals."

"They know it wasn't us, Andy," Carolyn said, trying to make him feel better. "They said it was probably a prank." She shook her head angrily as they started down the street. "A prank! Who in their right mind would do such a horrible thing?"

"Well, they didn't say whoever did it was in his right mind," Andy corrected her.

"It's sick," Carolyn muttered. "It makes *me* sick just thinking about it."

They walked several blocks in silence before Carolyn stopped and took his hand.

"I'm sorry, Andy. You're the one who found it in the first place. You're the one who got the shock."

"The worst shock was when I almost fell in," Andy said truthfully.

They looked at each other, and then they both burst out laughing.

"It's not funny," Carolyn insisted. "But if I don't laugh, I'll cry." She leaned up against a streetlamp and covered her face with her hands. "Why *now*, Andy? Why does this have to happen *now?* After everything else that's happened in that stupid house—"

"Oh, come on, it's a coincidence," Andy soothed her. "It doesn't have anything to do with you."

"And you really believe that?"

He grew quiet. He watched as she uncovered her face . . . as she gazed pleadingly back at him.

"Festivals always bring out the worst in people," he teased. "What do you bet it was a dare? Kids at a party or out riding around, having a little too much fun—hey, it could even have been some weird kind of scavenger hunt. It could have been *anyone's* grave they fooled around with—"

"But it wasn't," Carolyn said firmly. "They picked Carolyn's grave, and they must have picked it for a reason."

"Yeah. It's the one most isolated, the farthest back from traffic, and the least noticeable!"

She looked like she wanted to believe him but couldn't quite manage it.

"You really think so?" she asked.

Andy threw his hands up in the air. "Well, why else?

And if you mention ghosts one more time, I'll make you walk all the way home!"

This time she smiled. She leaned against him, and he felt her shiver.

"Cold?" Andy drew her close and hugged her.

"Sort of. But mostly just wondering where she is."

"Where who is?"

"You know," Carolyn said seriously. "Carolyn Glanton. Where is she now? Where did they take her?"

"God, you're morbid." It was Andy's turn to shiver now, and they started walking again. "There couldn't be much left of her, could there? I mean, it *has* been a long time—we're talking a century here, at least—"

"But they took her coffin, too."

"There probably *wasn't* a coffin. After all this time, it's probably gone. I have a feeling, whoever dug up that grave was really disappointed once they got in there." He gazed at her a minute, then shuddered again. "Can we not talk about this anymore, please? I'm going to have nightmares for a month."

Carolyn forced a smile, but her heart wasn't in it. She didn't want to ruin the rest of their day, but she couldn't stop thinking about Carolyn Glanton's grave. *Coincidence?* Andy's explanation made sense, she supposed, yet her own instincts told her something else—something dark and dangerous—something that made her suspicious and afraid.

"You game for the Ferris wheel?" Andy interrupted her thoughts, and Carolyn was surprised to see that they'd walked all the way to the carnival at the other end of the village.

She nodded and forced a smile. "If you are. I better warn you, though—Ferris wheels make me queasy."

Andy gave her a look of mock horror. "After what we just went through, what could make you queasier than that?"

"You're absolutely right," Carolyn said determinedly. "Let's go have some fun."

The rest of the day flew by. Andy kept Carolyn so busy that she didn't have time to think about grave robbers—or any of her other worries. By evening she was sure they'd ridden every ride, eaten at least one of every kind of food, inspected every single craft, tried their skill at every game, and walked at least a hundred miles back and forth through the village.

Exhausted, they found an empty table at a sidewalk café. Dusk was beginning to fall, but the festival continued around them, noise and laughter and music echoing through the shadows. One by one streetlamps blinked on, while colorful lanterns danced gaily above them in the night breeze. Carolyn yawned and stretched. She sipped her cappuccino while Andy leaned back in his seat and smiled at her.

"Happy?"

"I've had the best time. I don't want it to end."

"Well, you're in luck—it doesn't happen to end officially till tomorrow." His face brightened, and he leaned toward her. "Not only that, I've got a great idea. I'm taking a boatload of tourists out for a sunset cruise tomorrow evening. Why don't you come?"

Carolyn smiled and shook her head. "I don't know. I'll probably be too tired to do anything."

"It'll be beautiful," Andy promised. "You don't know what you're missing."

She laughed and finally nodded. "Okay. I'll think about it."

He looked so pleased that she reached over and took his hand. He moved even closer and bent his head against hers.

"Better be careful," he said in a dramatic whisper. "People might think we're involved."

Carolyn laughed again. "Well, we are sort of involved, aren't we—involved in some really strange things we didn't expect to—"

She broke off and sat rigid in her chair. Andy grimaced and tried to pry his hand out of her sudden grip.

"Ouch—hey—do you mind—I *need* that hand—"

"Andy, is that Joss?"

"What?" Andy wheeled around in his seat and tried to follow the direction of her gaze. "Where?"

"It looked like him," she insisted. "I could have sworn I saw him in front of that building."

Andy gave her a puzzled glance, then refocused his attention back across the street.

"Carolyn, I don't see a thing except about a hundred overweight tourists dancing to that stupid band over there. How in the world could you even recognize anyone?"

"It was him—I know it was."

"Well . . ." Andy's smile looked a little uneasy. "So maybe it *was* him. Is there some reason he shouldn't be out here if he wants to be?"

Carolyn snapped back to attention. "No, of course not. I just thought it was strange because he said he was working. That's all."

Andy's smile grew more perplexed. He looked up

into the sky and back to her. "Carolyn . . . it *is* dark out here now. There *is* such a thing as quitting time."

She shook her head. She squinted her eyes and tried to study the gyrating flock of tourists, but all she could see was a blur.

"You're right," she mumbled. "I probably didn't see him. Someone who just looked like him, maybe."

"What was he doing?"

"Watching us."

"Watching us?" Andy spun in his chair and strained once more through the darkness. "Why would he be watching us?"

"Andy, how should I know?" Carolyn's voice came out sharper than she intended. "I'm sorry, I didn't mean to snap. It's just that I thought he was there, and I thought he was watching us, and it makes me nervous."

"Well, he isn't there now," Andy soothed her, but there was a tinge of annoyance in his voice that hadn't been there before. "And he probably wasn't there to begin with. So will you calm down and finish your coffee?"

Carolyn nodded and lifted her cup. She held it to her lips without drinking it. Instead she stared over the rim and scanned the street corner one more time with narrowed eyes.

"Carolyn," Andy said gently, "come on, forget about it. If it really *was* him, maybe he just happened to see us here, and then he ducked out of sight so you wouldn't think he was staring."

Carolyn's frown was distracted. She swallowed the last of her cappuccino as Andy helped her up.

"I've got to get some change," Andy said, checking his wallet. "You want to wait here?"

"No, I think I'll go over there so I can hear the music better."

It was a lame excuse, and Carolyn knew it. She saw Andy give her a knowing look, but he only nodded and went into the café.

Carolyn crossed the street and stood on the edge of the curb. All around her people were laughing and dancing and keeping time to the music. She let her eyes roam slowly over each face, but not one looked even remotely familiar. She was just about to go find Andy again when a hand closed tightly around her elbow, sending her back with a startled cry.

"Molly!" Carolyn gasped. "Where did you come from!"

The strange little woman cocked her head, lips spread wide in a toothless sneer.

"I remember you," she mumbled, and she jabbed a crooked finger against Carolyn's arm. "Nervous you were, and asking questions. About the captain . . . about his silly, dead wife . . ."

"The hook," Carolyn said quietly. "You were telling me about the hook."

"People don't listen when they think you're crazy—"

"I don't think you're crazy, Molly," Carolyn insisted.

Molly's bulbous eyes rolled in her head. She lifted her hand and trailed it lightly down Carolyn's cheek.

"The face I remember. I do remember faces. And your name was the same as *hers*—"

"Yes, that's right. Carolyn."

"And my mind is going round and round. Ever since I saw you with your young man."

"My young man?" Carolyn looked blank. "What are you talking about?"

"I saw you there!" Molly pulled away and pointed toward the hill leading up past the library. "On the sidewalk. Talking to your young man—"

"Oh. Yes." Carolyn nodded uneasily. "His name's Joss. He's doing some work for us at the house—"

"Joss? *Joss?*" A thin thread of drool oozed down over Molly's whiskered chin. "I know that face, all right, but his name isn't Joss—it's—it's—"

"Joss," Carolyn said again, struggling for patience. "You couldn't know him, Molly, he just came to the island looking for work. That's why he's staying at our house for a while."

"But I've seen him before."

Carolyn stared at the glitter in Molly's eyes. The old woman's hand slid to her shoulder and clamped down, making her wince.

"It's your medicine, isn't it?" Carolyn said kindly. "We can talk again when you feel—"

"I've seen him," Molly whispered, "and I never forget a face. But *different* somehow. Yes . . . very different somehow . . . can't quite put my finger on it. . . ."

She shook her head and tugged on Carolyn's arm, leading her away from the crowd, over to another street corner that was quieter and completely deserted.

"Different," Molly mumbled to herself again.

"Different . . . different . . . but how? Same face. But something . . ."

Carolyn glanced back nervously, trying to find Andy in the crowds. Molly was still muttering, still pulling on Carolyn's arm.

"Ah, but I do know!" Molly suddenly hissed, and her mouth drew back in an empty grin. "And he's a sly one, isn't he . . . but not sly enough to fool old Molly!"

"What is it?" Carolyn was trying very hard to be patient, but Molly was pressing relentlessly on her shoulder blade now—really hurting her—and Carolyn was trying desperately to pull away—

"Yes, yes! Sly devil!" Molly's head bobbed up and down, but then suddenly she froze. "Psst! Hear that?"

Carolyn didn't hear anything except her own voice pleading. "Come on, Molly, why don't we go back? I'm waiting for—"

"Did you hear that?" Molly hissed, and she glanced back over her shoulder in obvious alarm. Carolyn looked, too, but saw only thick trees and shrubbery behind them.

Molly's mouth was a gaping black hole, silent words forming that Carolyn couldn't make out. Helplessly Carolyn shook her head.

"No, Molly, what are you saying? I don't understand—"

"Someone's watching," Molly hissed again. "Spirits, stay away from my soul!"

She whirled around, movements quick and birdlike. Her eyes nearly burst from her head as she stared into the leafy foliage. She picked up her shopping bag and gave the shrubbery a good sound whack, while

Carolyn covered her mouth and tried desperately not to laugh.

"Gone now," Molly breathed. "Someone *was* there, but now they're gone."

Carolyn didn't know whether or not to be scared. Taking Molly's hand, she finally managed to pull the old woman back along the sidewalk.

"Please, Molly, let's go back. It's too dark over here, and we might—"

"Blond!" Molly shrieked, and Carolyn shrank in embarrassment as people around them turned to stare. Molly was doing a strange little dance now, hopping from one foot to the other, switching her shopping bag from hand to hand. "Blond, blond— *blond!"*

"Molly—"

"I knew I'd remember, and I did!" Molly faced her defiantly, fairly spitting the words. "He had long fair hair when I saw him last! The night he walked with Hazel!"

Carolyn froze. She looked down at the old woman . . . watched as Molly's eyebrows drew deviously together.

"What . . . did you say?" Carolyn whispered.

"Hair the color of gold that night," Molly said smugly. "The color of sun in the dark! And him, pale as a spirit, and just as dead."

"What are you talking about?"

"The night he walked with Hazel by the sea."

"Please, Molly, you're not making any sense—"

"A secret admirer?" she cooed. "A long-lost beau? I saw them, but they didn't see me! Lured her there, he did—calling his own lost name! I hid behind the rocks, and I stayed a long, long time. And when I looked out again, *he* was walking back, but *she* wasn't."

"Molly . . . what are you . . . saying . . ."

The woman's fingers dug into Carolyn's arm. Her mouth moved close to Carolyn's ear, and the smell of rum nearly knocked Carolyn over.

"But *you* believe in ghosts, don't you, my dear?" Molly whispered. "Yes . . . yes . . . I do, too, because I *saw* one that night! *The ghost of Matthew Glanton!* In his long black coat, he was so tall and still with the wind blowing his hair, and for one quick second when the moon came out from the clouds, I could see his *face,* too, clear as I'm seeing yours! But he was *blond!* And today—when *you* were talking to him—he wasn't blond anymore!"

An icy chill shook Carolyn from head to toe. She pulled slowly from Molly's grasp and took a step back.

"You're lying." Carolyn shook her head, her words tumbling out faster than she could think. "You're lying to me—just trying to scare me—you really didn't see him before—you've *never* seen him before—"

"You've let him get close." Molly chuckled, and her laughter got louder and louder, her horrible fish-eyes only inches from Carolyn's nose. "Foolish, foolish girl! You'll never escape him now!"

19

SOMETHING ROARED THROUGH CAROLYN'S HEAD—
something wild and dangerous and frightening—yet
from some remote corner of consciousness, she knew
it wasn't the wind she heard, or the sound of the sea.
She started to say something to Molly, then realized
the woman was already out of sight over the top of the
hill.

"There you are!" Andy's voice brought her around
with a startled cry. "Hey, what's up? I was looking all
over for you."

He sounded so concerned that Carolyn reached out
and took his arm.

"Andy—"

"Don't wander off like that, okay? I was worried—"

"Andy, I was just talking to Molly—"

"No wonder you look upset. Did she try to sell you
something from her bag of tricks?"

Carolyn was shaking her head, tugging insistently
on his elbow. "Andy, she said something about Hazel

—about the night Hazel died. She was hiding on the beach and—"

"Hiding or passed out?"

Carolyn's smile was grim. "You were right about the drinking. She smelled awful."

"Molly's always on the beach. Molly's always seeing things."

"But she said she saw Matthew Glanton's ghost with Hazel and—"

Andy groaned and pried Carolyn's hand from his arm. "You're making me black and blue, Carolyn. I wish you'd stop beating me up every time you're trying to make a point." He chuckled and slipped his arm around her shoulders. "Yeah, yeah, I've heard that same story and so has the sheriff. And you can probably imagine how well it went over."

"You mean they didn't believe her?" Carolyn stared at him.

"Carolyn!" Andy stepped back, equally amazed. "Are you nuts? Who in their right mind would believe Molly? Her whole life consists of either sleeping or hallucinating! She doesn't even know the difference anymore between what's real and what's not!"

"But—" Carolyn floundered for words, for arguments. "Andy, she seemed so *sure!* I mean—"

"Sure. Uh-huh. About a ghost."

"But maybe *not* a ghost! Maybe what she *thought* was a ghost was a real person! And he had something to do with Hazel's death!"

Andy sighed. "Don't you think if Molly had any credibility at all, the sheriff would have thought of that already?"

172

"But, Andy—"

"Okay, can we talk about it in the car? I've got a really full day tomorrow, and *you* need to get some rest."

They'd started walking, but now Carolyn stopped and blocked his way.

Andy stopped, too, and groaned. "Now what?"

"Molly saw me talking with Joss today in front of the library—"

"Yeah? So?"

"She *recognized* him."

"What do you mean, she recognized him? Molly wouldn't recognize herself in a three-way mirror—"

"She said *he* was the one with Hazel that night. Except when she saw him, his hair was blond. And she kept calling him Matthew Glanton."

Andy stared at her. He stared at her for so long that Carolyn started to wonder if he'd completely tuned her out. Then suddenly Andy threw back his head and laughed.

"What's so funny?" Carolyn demanded, but it was several more seconds before Andy could catch his breath enough to answer.

"God, Carolyn, listen to yourself! Do you have any idea what Molly sees inside that mind of hers? Just last week she *swore* to Mr. Bell that all the sausages were glowing inside his meat counter—"

"I don't care about her other fantasies!" Carolyn insisted. "She seemed really serious about this!"

"She's always serious," Andy said, shaking his head. "Look, Carolyn, I already told you—Molly's crazy and everybody knows it."

"But that doesn't mean she didn't see *something* that night—"

"Yeah, okay, but in what other dimension?" Andy put his fists to his head, making a grunt of frustration deep in his throat. "Why are we even *having* this conversation! I think *I'm* losing my mind—"

"And when Molly told me all this stuff, I think Joss was hiding in the bushes listening to us."

This time Andy's face went dead serious. He leaned toward her, put a finger to his lips, and said in an exaggerated whisper, "No! Not in the bushes!"

"Well, someone was!" Carolyn defended herself indignantly. She shoved Andy back as he started laughing again. *"Someone* was watching us and hiding. *And* listening."

"Probably some poor guy who couldn't make it to the bathroom!"

"Andy, I heard the bushes *moving!* Someone was *there!"*

"Okay, okay, wait a minute." Andy nodded at her, deadpan. "Joss was hiding in the bushes listening to Molly tell you that he used to be blond when he was the ghost of Captain Glanton and killed Hazel. Right. I think I've got it all straight now."

Carolyn glared at him. The roaring was subsiding in her head now, and the street and the people and the colored lights were all coming back into focus.

"I want to go home," she said coldly.

She turned and hurried down the street, but she could hear Andy running behind her.

"Carolyn, wait—come back!"

Carolyn went faster. In another second Andy was at her side, and he grabbed her arm to turn her around.

"Okay, I'm sorry. But do you know how ridiculous this all sounds? It's getting crazier by the minute!"

"I'm just trying to make sense out of everything, Andy!" Carolyn flung back at him. "Molly said *I* was in danger—that I could never escape now!"

"Escape what?" Andy looked lost. "Escape *who?*"

Carolyn jerked away from him, but he went after her, talking as he tried to keep up.

"So what's going on in that mind of yours? So let's just say—for the sheer insanity of it—that Molly *did* see Joss that night. So why would he come *back* here?"

"I don't know. You tell me."

"Face it, Carolyn, it doesn't make any sense at all."

"That's just it—it *doesn't* make sense! *Nothing* makes sense! I'm trying to *make* things make sense, and you're not helping me!"

"What makes sense"—Andy drew a deep breath—"is that nobody killed Hazel and that nobody ever believes Molly."

Carolyn stopped so suddenly that Andy ran into her. She whirled back to face him, her face pale.

"You still don't get it, do you?"

"Get *what?*" Andy groaned.

"If Joss killed Hazel, then he just might have pushed my mother down the stairs. He just might have pushed me off the widow's walk. He just *might* be a homicidal maniac!"

"Oh, this is great. Just great! I can see it now—a houseful of plainclothes detectives to check out every guest at Glanton House! Just make yourself at home! While we run a police check and fingerprint you before you sign the guest book!"

"Take me home," Carolyn said tightly.

Andy stared at her. He started to reach for her hand, thought better of it, then walked around her, giving her a wide berth.

"Okay, fine. Think what you want. Better yet, why don't you just *ask* Joss if he killed Hazel. Or wait—this is better. While you're at it, ask him if he dug up Carolyn Glanton and what he did with her bones."

They didn't speak to each other all the way home. Andy let her off at the house, but Carolyn didn't wait for him to walk her to the door. Instead she hurried up the steps as Andy yelled from his open window.

"Does this mean our date's off for tomorrow?"

"I might not even be alive tomorrow!" Carolyn threw back at him. "This stupid house might *kill* me!"

"Then why are you going inside?"

Carolyn slammed the door. She stood for a moment staring into the shadows of the parlor, then she took a deep breath and walked farther into the room. A cozy fire crackled in the fireplace, and as her eyes grew accustomed to the light, she realized a lone figure was sitting in the rocking chair beside the hearth.

"Well," Joss said, "sounds like you had a wonderful time."

Carolyn opened her mouth . . . hesitated . . . shut it again. What was she going to do—come right out and confront him with her suspicions? Ask him about Hazel? Ask him why he was sneaking around the village today? *Good evening, Joss, and oh, by the way, were you spying on me tonight, were you thinking maybe of trying to kill me, and did you just happen to be on the beach the same time Hazel had her accident?*

"I don't know anything about you," she blurted out, and instantly regretted it. She couldn't see his face clearly, but she had the overpowering sensation that his eyes were boring into her, reading her thoughts, probing her very soul.

After a long silence Joss said, "There's not much to know."

"I thought I saw you in the village today," she said again before she could stop herself.

Joss sounded amused. "Hmmm . . . and I thought I was there. I thought you and I stood on the sidewalk and talked."

"I don't mean then. I mean later."

Shadows moved like liquid around him. His voice was deep and very soft.

"I've been working."

"Have you ever met Molly?"

"Who's Molly?"

"A bag lady who lives on the beach."

"No."

Carolyn stared at his silhouette and bit her lip in frustration. For one instant she could feel his kiss again . . . the strength of his arms . . . *So what's going on, Joss, and why were you so different then—*

"I'm going to bed."

"Good night," Joss said.

"If you need anything, you'll have to knock loud— I'm going to lock my door."

Again the shadows stirred, velvety blackness flowing around him like a dark, dark cape.

"That might be best," he murmured. "We wouldn't want any more accidents . . . would we?"

20

STUPID . . . STUPID . . . YOU PRACTICALLY CAME RIGHT
out and accused him—you practically admitted you
suspect him!

Carolyn was furious with herself.

She locked her bedroom door and leaned her head
against it, her heart pounding.

So transparent! I can't believe how obvious you were
down there—why didn't you just come right out and
ask him how he killed Hazel and how he made Mom
fall!

"Get a grip, Carolyn," she muttered to herself.
"Don't go over the edge on me now. . . ."

Like Hazel went over the edge . . . like Mom went
over the edge . . . like I almost went over the edge . . .

She turned and stared at her room. It blurred for a
moment through tears, and then it came into focus
once more.

But if he's a murderer, then why did he save me last
night?

She let her eyes wander slowly over the walls . . . the furniture . . . windows . . . her suitcase still propped open in the corner . . .

My suitcase.

Someone's been in my suitcase.

She didn't know why she thought so. She knelt on the floor beside it and very slowly, very carefully began pulling out her clothes—one by one—holding each thing up to the light and examining it closely for—*what? What am I looking for?*

She got to the end and put everything back. She sat there in the corner and let her gaze roam once more around the room. She'd made up her bed that morning, but now the covers looked rumpled and hastily smoothed. The pillow seemed slightly off center. The spread hung unevenly to the floor, as though someone had lifted it to look underneath.

Why would someone be in my room—what would they be looking for?

Carolyn was mystified. Her personal things hadn't even arrived yet—she'd hardly brought any clothes with her, much less anything of value that someone might want to steal. And she certainly didn't have anything with her that she might want to hide or lock away.

She crossed to her bed and sat down. It made her skin crawl just thinking someone else had been in here, searching through her things, maybe even sitting where she was sitting now. . . .

But it's just a feeling . . . I can't really prove anyone was in here. . . .

Uneasily Carolyn crawled into bed and clutched the covers to her chin. For a long, long while she hovered in that strange twilight state between sleep and wakefulness, and then finally she dreamed.

Voices were calling her—and the voices were the sea—and hands reached out from the waves, grabbing her arms and ankles, trying to pull her into the dark, churning water. She screamed, but no one heard. She tried to run, but the sand melted beneath her feet, pulling her down, swallowing her whole.

"No!"

Carolyn bolted upright in bed, her heart thudding. For the first few seconds, she looked wildly around her room, but then, as she realized it was just a nightmare, she huddled down under the blankets and tried to take deep, slow breaths.

She lay there wide-eyed, staring at the ceiling. There were no sounds from the third floor. No scratches, no clawing. No door banging back and forth in the wind. She raised up on her elbows and looked over at her windows. The wind was blowing fiercely, but there was no storm tonight. *Nothing to be scared about . . . nothing at all. . . .*

She got up. She pulled the flashlight from the nightstand drawer, and then she went to her door. She put her ear against it and listened. Everything on the other side seemed peaceful and still. After several moments she peeked out, then tiptoed into the hall.

Joss's door was open.

Startled, Carolyn peered through the doorway, trying to penetrate the thick shadows of his room. Her first thought was that he must have fallen asleep without shutting his door, but the longer she stood and listened, the more she came to realize that his room was empty.

"Joss?" she whispered.

No answer.

"Joss? Are you in there?"

She felt her feet moving noiselessly across the corridor . . . felt her hand lifting to knock. What came out was a soft tapping sound she could barely hear herself.

"Joss?"

Carolyn pushed the door all the way in. By squinting, she could just make out his bed beneath the window, and several other pieces of furniture scattered among the shadows.

But Joss wasn't there.

Carolyn glanced furtively over her shoulder. She scanned the hallway from one end to the other, her eyes lingering fearfully on the attic door. Everything seemed as it should be; she was quite alone.

She didn't know what she expected to find. She didn't even realize what she was planning to do until she was already standing in the middle of his room, playing her flashlight carefully across his bed. The covers hadn't been turned down for the night. There were no personal belongings anywhere.

She walked over to the bureau and pulled open the top drawer. Underwear. Socks. Hastily she closed it and went on to the next drawer—and the next. T-shirts. Shaving things. She slid the drawers back into place again and eased open the doors of the armoire. Just a couple of shirts. Not much to suggest he was planning to stay very long.

This is stupid—what am I doing anyway?

The thought suddenly came to her that Joss could

return at any second. And if he came in unannounced and found her snooping around . . .

She backed away from the armoire. She started past the bed again when she noticed something jutting out from under the spread, so she knelt down on the floor to investigate.

Books?

Carolyn aimed her flashlight onto the small stack, and then she frowned.

Yes . . . the books from the library.

She glanced over her shoulder, then very quickly began flipping through the volumes. Some of the pages had been turned down at their corners, and Carolyn looked them over carefully. To her disappointment, all she found were things she already knew—bits and pieces of local folklore and a rather nonsensical retelling of the legend of Glanton House.

The last book was nothing but pages and pages of names. Nothing in here seemed to be marked, but as she closed the book, her eye fell upon some writing scrawled on the inside back cover. She held her flashlight close and whispered them aloud.

"'Glanton. From England. Means a hill used by birds of prey, or as a lookout place.'"

Carolyn read the words again.

She read them again and yet again, and then she sat back on the floor and shook her head.

"Doesn't make sense," she murmured to herself. "Why would someone have written them down when they don't even make . . ."

And then . . . slowly . . . she felt her skin crawl.

She stared at the words and her heart quickened in her chest, sending little thrills of excitement all through her body.

"Lookout place . . . birds of prey . . ."

And in the back of her mind she was hearing Andy's voice again, on the very first day she'd met him, when he was talking about the island and its colorful history—

"Pirates . . . smugglers . . . hurricanes . . . shipwrecks . . . you name it, it's had them all . . ."

"My God," Carolyn whispered. "Matthew Glanton wasn't just an ordinary sea captain—he was a pirate!"

Her head was spinning. She read the words on the cover again, and her thoughts were flying thick and fast, so that she could barely keep up with them—

That must be it—that's got to be it! Matthew Glanton was a pirate and this was his lookout place, which means he must have brought cargo back here to unload and hide it—in caves maybe, along the coast, or even in this very house—treasure he got when he and his men preyed on helpless ships at sea—

And things were falling into place now, faster and faster, and Carolyn was so excited she could hardly hold the book in her trembling hands.

And Carolyn's lover must have known! And he only pretended to care about her, only pretended so he could find Matthew's treasure! He never counted on Matthew coming home again and ruining all his plans! But Matthew got his revenge—Matthew didn't die that night, just like Molly said—Matthew came back and killed them both—the man who tried to murder him, and the wife who betrayed him—

Carolyn put a hand to her heart. She felt positively

dizzy, and she leaned back against the wall, trying to get her thoughts under control.

Why hadn't Joss told her about the books? And why had he hidden them under his bed? *Pirates . . . murder . . . treasure—*

Something creaked in the hallway.

With a burst of terror Carolyn jumped up, dropping the book, and snapped off the flashlight.

Footsteps . . .

And they were coming this way.

Carolyn panicked. She hurried to the door, but it was already too late. There was no way she could escape now without being seen—no way she could get back to her own room before Joss came in and found her. Without a second's hesitation, she squeezed behind the bedroom door and flattened herself against the wall.

The footsteps were closer. In the terrifying silence they echoed down the corridor, pounded through her brain—and yet she knew they were no louder than a whisper, that they were approaching slowly . . . cautiously.

Carolyn clamped her eyes shut and prayed to be invisible. To her horror the door moved slightly. The footsteps froze just outside her hiding place.

Silence surged through the hall. It enveloped Carolyn like a net, choking her, squeezing each beat of her heart.

Through the cracks between the hinges, Carolyn saw a huge shadow looming over the door. She heard the faint rattle of the doorknob . . . felt the door inching slowly backward as she tried to mold herself even flatter against the wall.

Oh, please no . . .

The door stopped.

She didn't dare breathe. Her chest ached, and the blood froze in her veins.

The footsteps started again.

They moved across the hall and paused outside her bedroom, and Carolyn shut her eyes, trying to remember if she'd closed her door. After what seemed like forever, the steps moved on once more. She could hear them creeping toward the staircase, then they faded down to the floor below.

Joss . . . what are you looking for?

Carolyn willed herself to move. She summoned every ounce of strength and forced herself out of the bedroom, forced herself to creep to the top of the stairs where she could look into the hallway below. He'd already gone outside, and she knew he couldn't hear her now because the front door was still open and the wind was rushing in—yet still she tiptoed down, still she huddled there in the shadows, afraid to move, afraid he might step back in and see her there and—

A blast of wind caught the door, nearly crashing it against the wall. Carolyn stifled a scream and flung herself into a corner, watching in fear as a shadowy arm caught the door just in time and pulled it shut.

One final draft gusted through the room. It flared the embers in the fireplace and scattered them across the hearth.

And then without warning something swept across the floor and sailed straight into the fireplace.

Carolyn watched as a thin curl of smoke began to rise. She stared at the logs for several seconds before it dawned on her that a piece of paper had blown in on top of them. Running over, she snatched the paper out again just in time to save it from burning.

It had a jagged, irregular shape, as though it were torn, and a memory flashed back to her from that very morning—Joss coming into the kitchen, stuffing that paper into his pocket.

Carolyn inhaled slowly and held the paper nearer the light. It looked fragile and brittle. It was practically falling apart.

Someone had ripped it lengthwise, leaving only the ragged right-hand side of the page, but there were words still visible there, lettered in faded ink . . .

MY SECRET TREASURE
DARK
GRAVE DESPAIR
HOME
LIFE AND
DEATH
ETERNAL.

Carolyn lowered the paper and stared into the fire. *My secret treasure . . .*

Glanton House. A pirate's house . . . a house of murders . . . a house of mysteries . . .

For wouldn't a pirate's house have many secrets?

Secrets hidden? Secrets forgotten? *Valuable* secrets? Secrets locked away, so long, long ago?

"Locked away," Carolyn murmured. "With a key."

21

CAROLYN STOOD THERE BESIDE THE FIRE, STARING HARD into the flames, seeing nothing.

Treasure?

Was it possible? Treasure hidden somewhere in Glanton House?

Treasure that someone was trying to find because of this strange clue on this old torn piece of paper . . .

She sank down on the hearth, burying her face in her hands.

Treasure worth scaring people for?

Killing people for?

She couldn't stay down here. She had no way of knowing when Joss would come back and what he might do if he found her waiting. *I can't let him know . . . I can't let him know I've found this paper. . . .*

But surely he'd miss it. Surely he'd miss it and come searching for it sooner or later. *Just like he's been searching for the treasure. . . .*

The footsteps up and down the hall at night . . . the muffled tappings deep in the house . . . these pages marked in the library books . . . Now it was all starting to make sense to her. Joss must have been searching for treasure all this time—that's why he'd wanted this job so badly.

Again she held the paper up close, squinting at it in the shadows, and as she did so, Andy's words drifted back to her with new and terrible meaning. *"Nora said Hazel took in drifters now and then—word got around the docks that she'd give them work and a hot meal. They made Nora really nervous, so Hazel would call her up and tell her not to come if one of them was staying there. Nora never actually saw them. So who knows—maybe Hazel made them up."*

Carolyn lowered the paper to her knees. *Or maybe one of them was real—maybe one of them was Joss and maybe one dark night he disguised himself as Captain Glanton and lured Hazel to the cliffs—and now he's come back for the treasure, only this time Mom and I are in his way instead of Hazel. . . .*

Carolyn shuddered and rocked slowly back and forth, her arms wrapped tightly around herself, her heart heavy and sick. *He already knows I have the key . . . he was standing right there on the porch last night when I yelled at Andy—that's why I had that weird feeling about my room—he'd been in there looking around, and he followed me to the village today, too, and—*

Something creaked out on the porch, and Carolyn jumped to her feet. Panicking, she bolted for the stairs and ran to her room.

She locked the door and huddled behind it, listening for sounds from downstairs. She had that strange dreamlike feeling of standing off watching herself from some other person's body. The house was quiet. No sounds came from the first floor. *The paper . . . I've got to hide that paper. . . .*

She was afraid to turn on the light. She was sure the front door hadn't opened . . . sure that no one had entered the house, and yet she could almost feel eyes following her.

Almost as though someone were hiding and watching.

As though she weren't alone in her room.

She wondered where Joss was and when he'd be back. Tomorrow she'd run straight to the police. . . . She'd tell them all her suspicions about him. . . .

And you'll sound as crazy as Molly McClure, and you'll be the laughingstock of the island, just like Andy said.

Carolyn groaned and wondered what she was going to do. She had nothing but feelings to go on—feelings and doubts and no kind of proof whatsoever. The police couldn't do anything about Joss, except maybe force him to leave the house. *And then what if he comes back—and what if he did kill Hazel and do something to Mom's ladder and push me off the widow's walk—he's so good at making things look like accidents—*

"Stop," Carolyn hissed. "Stop it now!"

Her mind was going in circles; she wasn't thinking straight anymore. In darkness she groped her way to the bed and found her pillow, and then she slipped the note beneath it. She lifted the covers, but they felt heavy somehow, as though they were snagged on the other half of the mattress. Carolyn gave them a tug, then climbed in, burrowing down beneath the blankets.

Something was in her bed.

It was lying beside her, stretched out, lightly touching her back as she moved against it.

Carolyn froze. Her body went stiff, and her heart shot to her throat and stuck there, choking her, beating out of control.

Slowly . . . fearfully . . . she felt for the lamp and switched it on.

And at first it didn't register, the hideous thing lying next to her on the other pillow, *grinning* at her as she slowly rolled over and touched it, face to face. . . .

It had no eyes.

It had no flesh.

And as Carolyn screamed and screamed, the skull's mouth gaped open in a silent shriek of terror.

22

SHE DIDN'T KNOW WHAT SHE WAS DOING.

Carolyn flew downstairs and out of the house, racing blindly into the fog. She ran until she stumbled and fell, and then she lay on the ground, sobbing and beating her fists in despair.

She lay there for a long time.

Her gown was soaking wet, and she was chilled to the bone. No one came looking for her.

At last she sat up again, rubbing one muddy hand over her tear-streaked face. Her hair was damp and wild, and she was shivering uncontrollably. She thought about the skeleton in her bed, and suddenly she couldn't help it—she laughed out loud—a high-pitched sound that echoed hysterically all around her.

Somehow she knew that when she finally went back to her room, the grisly remains of Carolyn Glanton would be gone.

Gone without a trace . . . as if it had never been anything more than a dream.

Carolyn walked back to the house.

She climbed the stairs to her room, and she stood in her doorway and gazed silently at her bed.

And she was right.

23

THE ROOM WAS HAZY WITH MORNING LIGHT.

Stiff and groggy, Carolyn turned from her window and peeked cautiously out into the hall. Earlier, when she'd checked, Joss's door had been closed, but now it stood open, his room empty. Taking a deep breath, she went down to the kitchen. She sat at the table nursing a hot cup of coffee and concluded that she was indeed losing her mind.

So I dreamed last night, too—just like I dreamed the noises and the ghost in the attic and falling down the stairs. . . .

Except she hadn't been sleeping when she'd found that thing in her bed. And she hadn't slept the whole rest of the night, only sat there in the rocking chair, her mind numb and vacant.

She fingered the chain around her neck. She felt the thin outline of the key beneath her shirt.

But the body was there, and then it wasn't. So somehow I must have dreamed it. Just like I dreamed those footsteps in the hall ... and I guess I also dreamed—

The paper.

Starting up from the table, Carolyn remembered the torn piece of paper and how she'd put it under her pillow for safekeeping. She dashed back to her room and grabbed the pillow from her bed, running her hand along the sheet.

"Good morning," said a voice from the doorway.

Carolyn slammed the pillow onto the bed. Joss was standing there watching her, and she'd never even heard him coming. For a long moment he stared at her, and she stared back. Then slowly she straightened.

"Good ... morning," she forced out the words.

"How'd you sleep?"

Carolyn stared at him, her heart thudding. *He knows ... he knows everything ... he knows I was in his room last night—that I heard him out in the hall—that I've found his paper—*

"Are you okay?" Joss lifted an eyebrow.

But of course he doesn't know—he's not a mind reader—how could he possibly know—

"Yes, I slept fine." *There's nothing under my pillow —the paper's gone—*"Just fine. Thanks."

He nodded. "You want some breakfast?"

But that's impossible—it can't be gone—I remember putting it right here last night before I found that—

She shook her head. "I ... I made coffee earlier, but I'm not very hungry right now."

Did I dream that part about the pillow, too? Or did someone really take the note? Just like someone took that dead thing from my bed—

"I smelled it when I woke up," Joss said, and Carolyn jumped.

"Smelled what?"

"The coffee. Is something wrong?"

"No. Of course not." *Did you sneak into my room and did I really fall asleep in the chair, only I never knew it—*"Why?"

"You look a little funny, is all."

"No." She smiled. "No. Like I said, I'm really okay. I'm just . . . you know. Making the bed."

Joss gave her a puzzled glance and left. She heard him go down to the kitchen. Standing there in confusion, Carolyn felt as if she was going to start screaming any second and would never be able to stop.

Calm down . . . calm down . . . this is crazy . . . don't jump to conclusions.

Carolyn went through every piece of furniture in her bedroom . . . examined every inch of her purse . . . her clothes . . . even her shoes. She forced herself to strip the bed and shake out every cover, then she balled everything up for the laundry.

No paper. Nothing.

She stood for a long time gazing out the window into the gray, desolate morning. And then finally she turned around and went downstairs.

Joss was at the kitchen counter sipping from his coffee cup.

"Where's Nora?" he asked as Carolyn walked in. "Isn't she usually here by now?"

"Maybe . . ." Carolyn took a deep breath. "Maybe she slept in this morning. Maybe she was tired."

Joss acknowledged this with a vague nod. "Have you called the hospital yet? Talked to your mom?"

Yes, I already called the hospital very early when I first came down—or was that yesterday—no, I'm sure it must have been an hour or so ago—wasn't it?

"She's feeling better. But they still don't know exactly when she can come home. It may be another week yet."

"Are you going to see her today?"

"She told me not to. She said it wouldn't be worth the long drive there and back again just to be able to stay for an hour."

Again he nodded. She watched his eyes lift . . . settle on her face. Two coal black mirrors with no reflections.

"It probably won't be too much longer, though," she said stupidly. "That she can come home, I mean."

"Isn't that great," he murmured.

Carolyn stared at him. His face was expressionless.

"Did . . ." She swallowed hard and tried to keep her voice casual. "Did you hear any weird noises last night?"

Joss turned his back to her. He seemed to be looking at something out the window, but all Carolyn could see out there was fog.

"What kinds of noises?" he asked softly.

"I don't know. Something woke me. I got up, but you weren't in your room."

He was silent a moment. "What were you doing in my room?"

Carolyn thought quickly. "I wasn't in your room—the door was open."

Still he said nothing. She sat at the table and twirled her cup between her palms. Her coffee was ice cold.

"Anyway"—she sighed—"I guess it was just the wind."

She didn't expect any comment. So it surprised her when he said, "I took a walk."

"A walk?"

"Yes. Late. That must have been where I was when you tried to find me."

Again she made her voice casual . . . so carefully, carefully casual. "In the dark? In the fog?"

"I was"—he smiled faintly—"looking for ghost lights."

Carolyn watched his back, the set of his shoulders. "And did you find any?"

Joss didn't answer. He tossed his coffee into the sink.

"I've got work to do," he said.

The day dragged endlessly. Nora arrived in her usual sullen humor and disappeared upstairs. Carolyn wandered restlessly through the house, starting at every sudden noise. She watched the road and listened for the phone, wishing she and Andy hadn't argued, wishing he'd get in touch with her. She was certain that if she didn't get out of the house soon, she'd explode. She finally decided to drive to the village herself, but when she went out to the car, she found Joss under the hood, where he informed her that the car wouldn't run.

Uneasily Carolyn went back into the house, pausing to gaze at distant clouds. It looked like rain, and the air held that tense expectancy of something unknown about to happen. She decided to tackle the brochure Mom had been planning. She sat down at the kitchen table and tried to think of ways to make Glanton House sound inviting.

The hours crawled by. She realized she hadn't heard sounds of Joss working and wondered nervously where he was. Nora left for the day. The wind blew harder around the eaves of the house, and the rooms grew damp and chilly. Checking the parlor, Carolyn found the fire almost out and the woodpile down to nothing on the hearth.

The house loomed around her, sad and secretive. *I've got to get out of here—I can't stand it anymore.*

After slipping on her jacket, she headed off toward the cliffs. The wind reddened her cheeks and tossed her hair, piercing through her clothes with bitter intensity. *Driftwood,* she thought suddenly. *I'll get some driftwood to use in the fireplace.*

She was more careful this time, moving along the rocky overhangs. Out over the water dusk was gathering, the darkening sky churned by angry clouds. Carolyn tilted her face up, wishing for warmth, but feeling only the wet wind of a brewing storm.

She found the path without too much trouble. Far below the beach was still littered with chunks of wood and trails of seashells and clumps of seaweed tangled on the outcroppings of rocks. Carolyn pressed herself against the cliff wall and started down.

She could hear the rhythmic call of the sea, the giant waves rushing and receding, and each time they smashed against the sharp rocks, a fine spray of salt settled around her like a cloud. Wiping her cheeks, she hunched her shoulders against the wind and tried not to think about the awesome power of the ocean.

The steps seemed narrower today—steeper

somehow—slimy and slippery with spray. Holding her breath, Carolyn tried to grip the escarpment as she went down, but her fingers slid uselessly away. It was hard to keep her balance, and it seemed to take hours to make the descent. The view down made her dizzy, yet at the same time she felt a peculiar exhilaration as she finally touched bottom.

She came out into the cove and stood for a moment looking around. She could see the little pocket of beach tucked back beneath overhanging cliffs, bordered by a jagged row of rocks which rose several yards out to sea. Waves crashing against the breakfront spewed over the barrier and drenched her to the skin. Shivering, she began to pick her way among the driftwood, choosing the biggest pieces she thought she'd be able to carry.

She worked as quickly as she could, moving off along the beach, keeping one eye nervously on the clouds. She hadn't walked this far last time, and as she followed the rugged line of coast, she suddenly realized how quickly the fog was rolling in—not wisps of it, but great gray waves—rapidly cutting her off from the rest of the world.

Carolyn stopped, anxiously scanning the ocean. The waves had been growing more restless as she walked, but now one in particular began to lift itself up to alarming proportions and hurl toward her. Carolyn turned and ran back, scrambling around a jutting section of cliff wall.

She didn't expect to see someone else there on the beach . . . the figure standing half in shadows, gazing down at something sprawled across the rocks. . . .

Joss turned around as she came up behind him.

Turned with a quick look of shock and surprise, and then took a step backward, so that she could really see now, the thing lying there at his feet . . .

The throat was ripped open—flesh and bone and lungs scooped out—a gory, bloody mess . . .

Yet Carolyn still recognized the face.

She recognized it as it gazed up at her through long silvery hair and clumps of seaweed, and as she turned away, her stomach heaved violently, and she cried over and over again—

"Molly—oh, God—Molly . . ."

24

"CAROLYN!"

"Get away from me, Joss! Don't come any closer!"

Carolyn stumbled backward and nearly fell. She could see him moving toward her, his eyes dark and narrowed—and behind him she could still see what was left of Molly McClure.

"Carolyn, don't be stupid—I found her like this—"

"Like you found my mother? Like you found me in the attic? Like you found Hazel before you killed her?"

"Hazel? What the hell are you talking about?"

Overhead the sky exploded with lightning. Carolyn felt rain on her face, and she lifted her voice above a burst of thunder.

"Molly saw you that night, and that's why you had to shut her up, isn't it? Because you're back again, and she recognized you."

"What are you *talking* about?"

Joss strode toward her, his hands outstretched as though to calm her down. Glancing wildly around, Carolyn spotted a huge chunk of driftwood and grabbed it.

"I'll use this if I have to—I swear I will—now *stop!*"

Joss did. He shook his head, cheeks flinching in anger.

"Something's going on here, Carolyn, but I'm not the one you should be worried about—"

"I'm not going to listen to you anymore! I'm going to call the police!"

"No, wait! Don't go back to the house!"

But Carolyn turned and ran. Behind her she could hear the thud of his feet on the sand, and then he had ahold of her arm, trying to turn her around. Screaming, she managed to pull out of his grasp. As Joss wrestled her for the club, she jerked it free for a split second and swung it hard into his ribs.

She heard him gasp—saw him stagger. Dropping her weapon, she wheeled away, but he grabbed her from behind, and they both pitched into the water. Carolyn lashed out at him as he tried to pin her arms. She felt a sting at her neck, and sand ground into her skin.

"Stop it, Carolyn—just listen to me!" Joss began, but again she managed to wriggle out of his grasp and sprinted up the beach.

The rain was pouring now, the sky as black as midnight. Carolyn kept running, terrified he would follow, not knowing where she was headed. As she put distance between them, she kept waiting for him to chase after her, but when nothing happened, she finally slowed down to catch her breath.

She had no idea where she was—how far she'd gone.

As she flattened herself against the face of the cliff, she gazed back at the winding stretch of jagged coastline and saw only a hazy outline beneath billowing layers of fog. Panic went through her, but she forced it away, reminding herself she couldn't get lost as long as she followed the shore. Straining her eyes through the heavy mist, she thought for one second that she might have seen Joss in the far, far distance, but then he disappeared into the shadows, leaving her alone.

I've got to get back to the house—I've got to call the police—

Once more she started off, trying to find the path that would lead her up the cliff to safety. She didn't want to admit she was lost—didn't want to admit she must have passed her house long ago—totally disoriented now in a maze of fog and rain and shadows.

She never expected to see a light.

Just the faintest flicker . . . a quivering blur through the darkness.

Ghost light . . .

Carolyn watched it, too terrified to move. It glimmered weakly . . . faded . . . came to life again—and for one split second she could almost feel ghostly arms clutching her with cold, dead fingers. She tried to scream but couldn't. The light moved sideways, then back, bobbing through the fog.

Slowly Carolyn followed it.

Exhausted, soaked through to her skin, she felt

herself moving closer and closer, drawn by some hideous curiosity. As she drew near to it at last, it suddenly sputtered and went out.

Carolyn stared in disbelief. She couldn't have imagined it—it had been there only a second before. Fighting back panic, she flung herself toward it and came face to face with a solid wall of rock.

Of course—a cave!

Her heart raced in her chest. Pressing her hands against the rock, she felt her way along for several feet, then froze as sounds floated eerily out to her through the fog.

"You shouldn't have lost that paper! That half of the note was all we had—"

"Forget the paper—I know it by heart anyway."

Carolyn felt a wave of giddiness wash over her. She could see the mouth of the cave now—a yawning black hole throbbing with light and shadow from within. She could see the wooden crates heaped around the entrance . . . and even with the wind and rain and crash of the sea, she could recognize the voices that were arguing.

"Suppose *she* finds the paper!" Nora snapped. "Suppose she finds the treasure!"

"We've practically torn that house apart, and *we* can't even find it!" Andy threw back.

They both sounded angry. As the storm raged louder around her, Carolyn could only pick out bits and pieces of their conversation.

"I want her gone," Nora said. "Joss—"

Thunder drowned out the rest. Flattening herself against the rock, Carolyn crept closer, straining to hear. The crates blocked her way, so she carefully climbed on top of them, leaning as close as she could to the entrance.

"—going to find that treasure—last thing I do!" Nora's voice rose sharply. "—captain hid—somewhere in the house—worth a fortune!"

Andy faded back in. "—more important things to worry about."

"—not my fault they wanted this shipment tonight!" Nora's tone was icy. "—not my fault—wasn't planned—wasn't part of the schedule, but I always come through, don't I? Not like some—"

"If you mean Molly, it's your own fault she's starting to talk again. How many times have I told you, you can't depend on her to keep her mouth shut—even if she *is* full of rum and pills—"

Another crash of thunder cut through their discussion. Frustrated, Carolyn inched closer. Andy and Nora were sounding more agitated by the minute, and their shadows quickened along the entrance to the cave.

"And wouldn't everyone be shocked to know she's your sister?" Andy gave a sharp laugh. "—touching the way you look after her. Blood thicker than water and all that—"

"Shut up and work!" Nora yelled. "The boat's coming—eleven. We've got all these guns to move by then—expecting shipment—Canada—morning—"

"Don't worry. They'll get their shipment—always do."

"—getting too dangerous. I want her taken care of, understand?—not going to wait anymore—"

"Be patient," Andy snapped at her. "Carolyn's tough—but she's not impossible."

"—just the thing to break her," Nora said.

Fear pounded sickeningly through Carolyn's veins. As shadows moved across the cave entrance, she gasped and drew back just in time. Andy hurled a crate out onto the sand. Nora stood just behind him, her dark hair loose around her gaunt face, dressed in pants and a bulky sweater. As the thunder subsided for one brief instant, Carolyn pressed back into the shadows and heard clearly what they were saying.

"Just what did you have in mind?" Andy asked.

And Nora laughed . . . a horrible, frightening sound that made Carolyn's blood run cold.

"Why, Joss, of course. After all . . . with him dead, who'll be there to save her?"

25

THEY MOVED BACK INTO THE CAVE.

As Carolyn slowly unmolded herself from the rock, she could hear Andy and Nora talking again, but she couldn't make out what they were saying.

For a long time she just stood there.

They're smuggling guns to Canada.

They're looking for the captain's treasure.

Her breath caught in her throat, and she gave a sob.

They're going to kill Joss.

With a sinking heart, she remembered the horrible sound her club had made as she'd swung it into Joss's side.

I've got to find him . . . I've got to warn him!

Carolyn stood helplessly, her eyes straining through the darkness. *Which way did I come from? Which way should I go?* Preparing to jump down, she took a step backward. Without warning, several of the crates shifted beneath her and turned over, throwing her headlong across the pile. There was a crash as she landed, and then to Carolyn's horror, the sounds of running from inside the cave.

Scrambling up, Carolyn bolted.

She raced through the rain and fog, stumbling across the wet sand, splashing through the waves as they roared and crashed upon the shore. Shadows smothered her, swirling around her like lost phantoms. The wind shrieked and moaned, and the cliffs rose up and up, blocking all hope of escape. She wanted to scream Joss's name, scream for help, but she didn't dare, for fear that Andy or Nora would hear her.

Joss has to still be there—please let him still be there—

An image of Molly's face rose into her mind—the bulging eyes, the horror in that glazed stare—and *I'm sorry, Joss, I didn't know—I didn't know—*

Carolyn stopped, looking around in confusion. Nothing was even remotely familiar—she couldn't even see the water anymore, though from the sound of it, she knew it was dangerously close.

She fought down panic. Could she have already passed the spot where she'd seen Joss and Molly? Surely not, it had seemed so far away. . . .

Stop it . . . calm down. All she had to do was find the cliffs; all she had to do was follow the curves and angles around the shoreline. Then she'd find Joss. Then she'd find the cliff path that would take her back to the house where she could call for help. . . .

The beach glowed eerily as lightning burst over the water. Thunder rumbled, and the rain began to beat harder.

Carolyn turned in a slow circle, desperately trying to think. *Oh, Joss, where are you?*

Then suddenly he was there.

Shadowy . . . formless as fog . . . he materialized from the darkness and stood blocking her path. With a scream Carolyn jumped back, then stared at him in amazement.

"Joss! We've got to get out of here, we've got to call the police! Do you hear me? They're going to do something to you—Andy and Nora—I heard them say so, only they didn't know I was listening—"

And he was closer now, she could see the long sleeves of his sweater, and his hair blowing wild and dark across his face, and suddenly she felt his hands on her arms and they started to tighten . . . slowly . . . slowly . . . until his grip was unbearable, and she struggled but couldn't get free—

"Stop it!" she cried. "Joss, stop it! You're hurting me!"

But it wasn't Joss's voice that laughed as something slammed hard against her skull . . . that laughed and laughed as the fog rushed thickly, mercifully through her brain—

"Don't be silly, Carolyn," Nora scolded. "Joss would never hurt you."

26

"I DON'T SEE THE POINT OF BRINGING HER HERE," NORA fumed, knotting rope around Carolyn's ankles. "We should have just thrown her into the sea and been done with it." She gave one last tug, watching in satisfaction as Carolyn winced from the pain.

On the other side of the room Andy barely looked at them.

"I thought the whole idea was *not* to attract attention to the beach," he said tersely.

He lifted the lantern he was holding, jaundiced light flickering over the musty walls of the attic. From somewhere behind him fine sprays of rain misted in, and as a burst of thunder shook the house, his eyes briefly met Carolyn's before he turned away.

"She'll be safe here," he added. "At least till we decide what to do with her."

"Safe?" Nora gave a hoarse laugh. "Why keep her safe when we're going to kill her anyway?"

Carolyn went rigid. Lying there on the attic floor,

if it weren't for me, you'd have plenty of interference on your hands. You're lucky everyone around here's so superstitious. With the poor dead captain calling out his name . . . and the occasional ghost light on the beach . . . the islanders keep far away from this place."

He shifted in the doorway, one arm gesturing toward the night beyond. Carolyn heard him laugh, a dry, humorless sound.

"Of course, they'd be really disappointed to find out poor Matthew's just a recording. And the souls of his drowned sailors, just plain ordinary lanterns. It's always so tragic, isn't it, Nora, when people find out their legends aren't real."

"The treasure *is* real," Nora snapped. "We've looked this long for it, we can't stop looking now just be—"

She broke off abruptly as a strange tapping sound echoed softly through the room.

"What's that?" With one quick motion Andy stepped back into the shadows, his body poised to attack.

For an endless moment no one moved.

The tapping came again . . . more insistent this time. Without warning a low groan vibrated from the floorboards to the rafters, and as everyone watched in amazement, a section of the wall began to slide open. A second later Joss stepped out into the attic, a tall gray phantom covered with dust and cobwebs.

Nora was speechless. She gaped at him as Andy moved out into the light.

"You were right, Nora," Joss said quietly. "The treasure *does* exist. And I just found it."

Reaching behind him, he slowly withdrew something from the dark chasm of the wall. Then he rubbed at it with the sleeve of his sweater and held it into the sputtering light.

"My God," Andy breathed, "it's a *hook!*"

From her spot in the corner Carolyn stared in awe. The thing was huge—much larger than a man's hand—and the base was covered with jewels. At its opposite end the hook section curved gracefully to a fine, thin, razor-sharp point. Even beneath layers of age and grime, a sheen of gold showed through, and as Nora's hand shot out, Joss pulled the hook away from her.

"*You!*" Nora fairly spat at him. "But this is *impossible*—how could you—"

"The key," Joss said calmly. "And Molly."

Nora's face contorted. Her hands clenched into fists, and she stepped away from him, her voice low and shaken. "I don't *believe* you!"

"Solid gold," Andy murmured. "And those are emeralds . . . diamonds . . . rubies—this thing must be *priceless!*"

But Joss didn't seem to hear. His gaze had settled on Carolyn, and as she stared back in disbelief, his eyes flicked immediately to Andy.

"What's this?" Joss demanded, nodding in her direction.

Andy seemed reluctant to answer. His shrug was almost defensive.

"She saw us down on the beach. We had to bring her."

"I . . . see," Joss mumbled, and as Carolyn watched the knowing looks on their faces, she felt icy stabs of fear and confusion deep, deep inside her.

Her hands worked frantically at the ropes. Warm trickles of blood oozed over her wrists, but she kept her face expressionless and tried to concentrate on what Nora was saying.

"After all this time," Nora murmured. Her eyes narrowed in on the hook again, as though she still couldn't believe what she was seeing. "All my hard work . . ."

"You didn't tell me about the note, Nora," Joss chided, and his voice was unsettlingly calm. "You didn't tell me you had half of a message that could make you a very rich woman . . . and that it wasn't any use to you without the other half. I might never have known about it at all if it hadn't been for Carolyn's mother."

He held the hook in front of his face. He squinted at the jeweled handle, then slowly lowered it.

"That day she fell," he went on, remembering. "She'd been cleaning and moving furniture, and she must have come across the note hidden somewhere in that bedroom. The paper was in her hand when I found her."

Paper—paper! Carolyn's mind reeled. *That day at the hospital, Mom was trying to tell me, but I thought she was talking about an ad for the guest house—*

"So you kept it," Nora's voice was carefully controlled. "And all this time I was looking for it . . . *searching* for it . . ."

Joss said nothing. Again he held the hook up, watching the play of lantern light along its deadly point.

"Actually you made it easy for me at the end." Joss's lips moved in a half smile. "The night Andy planted the skeleton in Carolyn's room, he lost the note, didn't he? Carolyn must have found it when she followed him downstairs . . . and later, when I took the skeleton away, I found the note under her pillow."

Carolyn felt stunned . . . dreamlike. She could hear Joss talking, but he seemed miles away. *So you were in on it, you were helping them all the time. . . .*

"Shall I go through the whole message?" Joss asked.

He gazed into Nora's furious stare. Then he began to recite.

"'To you who shall unearth my secret treasure . . . where I lie waiting in the dark . . . remember only that love builds walls of grief and grave despair . . . that leave a man hollow of heart and home . . . and yet one key unlocks this mystery of life and death . . . and truth eternal.'"

No one spoke. Thunder rumbled the floor beneath them, and rain beat savagely against the roof.

"So *we* had the secret treasure part"—Andy gave a wry smile—"and *you* had the part about the key."

Joss nodded slowly. "And Carolyn had the *real* key."

Carolyn felt three pairs of eyes upon her. She lifted her chin defiantly and stared back at them.

"She tried to tell you, Andy, that night you brought her home," Joss continued. "But you didn't hear her, and Nora didn't understand what it meant."

So you were the one going through my room, Carolyn thought miserably. *You were the one all along. . . .*

"I didn't know where it was until tonight," Joss spoke again. "Until Carolyn's necklace broke."

When I fought with you on the beach . . . when I accused you of killing Molly . . .

"So you put the clues together," Andy picked up. "You already had 'love builds walls' and 'hollow' and 'one key unlocks this mystery and truth'—"

Joss shook his head. "But I still hadn't figured it out. Molly helped me do that."

"Molly?" Nora looked positively gray. "How . . . how could Molly have helped you?"

Joss looked her full in the face. "Exactly, Nora," he said quietly. "How could she?"

His stare was so hard and so terribly cold that even Nora took a step back from him.

"She was pointing straight to it when I found her." Joss gave a grim smile. "That disgusting excuse for a house down there on the beach. On the inside wall of the cave next to where she slept. She must have known all along there was a keyhole there, but she wasn't about to tell *you.*" He indicated Nora with a scowl. "It's a door to a tunnel, and the tunnel leads here."

"But there are lots of tunnels attached to this place," Andy spoke up while Carolyn listened in astonishment. "All to the cellar—they've been there for over a hundred years."

"But this one leads farther," Joss explained. "It's the only one that leads *up.* Don't you see? If anyone ever suspected the captain of smuggling, they'd naturally look for tunnels in the cellar. But this tunnel went *up!* Behind false walls all the way to the attic!"

Andy looked stunned. "Then . . . the captain—"

Joss gestured toward the open wall behind him. "What's left of him is in there. He must have carried out his revenge . . . then walled himself up to die."

Nora's hand plucked at the neck of her sweater. Andy gazed at the wall, then abruptly turned back to the widow's walk.

"Well, then . . . " Nora's voice sounded unnaturally loud in the sudden stillness of the room. "Now that our little treasure hunt is over, I believe there's some unfinished business we need to take care of."

"Which is?" Joss prompted.

She met his eyes boldly, one hand gesturing at the corner where Carolyn was still trying to free herself.

"Oh, come now, Joss—you don't really believe we can let her go after what she's heard tonight?"

Andy ducked his head. He looked nervous, and as Carolyn watched in growing fear, he shifted from one foot to the other and ran both hands back through his hair.

"About Molly," he burst out, though he wouldn't look at Joss. "What exactly do you mean . . . when you *found* her?"

"What does Molly have to do with anything?" Nora objected, but Joss took a step toward Andy, a muscle clenching in his cheek.

"Molly's dead," Joss said quietly.

This time Andy whirled to face him. Even in the dim lanternlight, he looked abnormally pale.

"What?"

"You heard me. I found her down on the beach with her throat torn out. Chalk up one more murder to the dear old captain, right, Nora?" Joss's tone was bitter, but Nora only smiled.

"It was only a matter of time, you both *knew* that—"

"You said no more accidents, Nora," Andy broke in angrily. "You said we'd be able to scare them away—you said—"

"She was getting careless." Nora's eyes narrowed into an ice-cold stare. "I didn't want you getting caught, Andy, that's all. I was only thinking of your safety."

"And I was only thinking," Joss broke in, his eyes locked with Andy's, "how easy it's getting to dispose of people."

"Inconveniences," Nora corrected him. "We can't have people snooping around here, getting in our way!"

Joss was pacing now, eyes lowered to the hook in his hands. His voice was low and thoughtful.

"I think I'm beginning to understand about these inconveniences, Nora. Like former employers, maybe?"

"*That* was pure genius," Nora gloated. "Having Andy masquerade as the captain . . . luring Hazel out to the cliffs . . ."

Carolyn caught her breath as another realization suddenly hit her. *Andy!* That day outside the library, when Molly had insisted she recognized the captain— *I'd been talking to Andy then, not Joss—*

"And one push from you." Joss gave a faint smile. "One problem solved." His eyes flicked briefly to Andy. "Or did *you* do the honors?"

"I didn't kill anybody!" Andy protested. "Nora—"

"And Mrs. Baxter was easy, too, wasn't she?" Joss went on. "You knew she was planning to go through those closets that day, didn't you, Nora? So you had that broken ladder all ready for her to use."

"I *could* have killed her," Nora said smugly. "But I didn't."

Carolyn squirmed desperately, trying to shout through her gag. She pushed herself away from the wall and lay there on her stomach, but all attention was on Joss.

"And then there was the widow's walk," he murmured.

He'd stopped pacing. Now he turned slowly and stared into Nora's face.

"We all agreed there'd be no real danger, didn't we?" he went on softly. "Another ghost, maybe . . . but nothing fatal."

Nora stared back at him. Her face looked hideous in the flickering light of the lantern.

"Carolyn almost died," Joss said flatly.

"But thanks to you, of course she didn't." A smile tightened Nora's lips, and she glanced at Andy. "We're both so proud of you, Joss. Your job was to work inside the house . . . become a trusted part of the family . . . scare them into leaving. To follow orders, no questions asked. And you've done your job so well. But now . . . you understand . . . all jobs have to end sometime."

Andy straightened in slow motion, but Carolyn caught the quick look of panic on his face. As Nora raised her gun, a shaft of lightning exploded outside the window, bathing everything in a silvery glow. Nora turned the gun on Carolyn.

"I'm an excellent shot," Nora said. "So give me the hook, Joss."

Joss didn't take his eyes from her. As he started forward, Nora seemed to change her mind.

"No. Put it there on the floor. Andy . . . tie his hands."

Joss leaned over with exaggerated slowness and put the hook down. Without a word, Andy pulled Joss's arms behind his back, securing them with a length of rope.

"Now . . ." Nora said, pleased. "Tie our friends together." At Andy's look of surprise, she added, "I think a touch of romance is in order . . . in keeping with the legend, you understand."

This time Andy hesitated. His glance shot from Joss to Carolyn and back again.

"Do it," Nora hissed.

"I'm not going to kill them," Andy said flatly. "I mean it, Nora—I won't—"

"Of course not. We'll let the house do it."

Keeping the gun aimed at Carolyn, Nora reached down for the lantern on the floor beside her.

"A fire, I think," she murmured. "With the money from this treasure, we won't be needing this place anymore . . . or the business."

She lifted the lantern with her free hand. Her eyes glittered wickedly in the gloom.

Andy motioned to Joss. At first Joss didn't move, but as Nora clicked back the hammer of her gun, he finally crossed the room. Andy stepped over Carolyn and shoved Joss roughly against the wall behind her.

"Lie down," Nora ordered.

Slowly Joss did so, putting his back to Carolyn.

"No," Nora said. "Face to face, so you can't untie each other. Besides . . . I want you to see each other at the end."

Carolyn's heart raced out of control. As Andy

forced her onto her side, she tried to kick him, but he sidestepped easily. Joss stretched out next to her with his back to the wall, and Andy pushed the two of them against each other.

"What are you doing?" Nora demanded, and Andy's reply was just as terse.

"Tying their knees together. There's no way they can reach the rope down there."

Nora seemed satisfied. As Carolyn watched in growing terror, Andy worked the rope around their legs, and yet strangely enough, it didn't feel tight. She saw Joss glance up at him . . . caught the quick, almost indifferent glance Andy threw back. Then Andy straightened and moved away.

Carolyn was almost afraid to breathe. Pressed lengthwise against Joss, she was helplessly aware of their bodies molded together, the warm strength of him through their wet, clinging clothes. Her head rested just beneath his chin. She felt his lips move gently against her hair. Tilting her face, she saw him looking down at her, his eyes deep and black and calm. She felt herself flush and lowered her head.

"It'll be quick," Nora promised with a laugh. "This attic is like a tinderbox. It'll be over before you know it."

"And you really think you'll get away with it," Joss spoke up, his tone strangely amused. His deep voice sent vibrations through his chest, beneath Carolyn's cheek. "You really think no one will ever suspect."

"Why should they? When I left here this evening, everything was fine. Accidents do happen."

"But two employers, Nora? *Two* accidents?"

"She's right," Andy broke in quickly. "No one's

going to think anything about this old place burning up."

He stepped in front of Nora, standing between the lantern and the corner where Joss and Carolyn lay. Carolyn felt Joss stir slightly, his body shifting along hers. She drew her breath in as he squirmed carefully in the shadows.

"Maybe so, Andy," Joss said casually. "But I can't help but wonder when *your* accident will happen."

Without warning Carolyn felt the ropes loosen around her knees. As Joss shifted again, his hand lightly patted her leg, and with a shock, she realized he'd gotten untied.

She'd never been so frightened.

And yet, in some strange way, she felt remarkably calm.

Lying there, she looked into Joss's face and slowly nodded to show him she understood. Then she steeled herself for whatever might happen next.

"Go on, Andy," Nora said.

Andy hesitated . . . glanced back to the corner.

"I said go on," Nora said, her voice hardening. "Or Carolyn gets to die now while both of you watch."

She waited while Andy moved to the stairs. Her aim was focused and steady on Carolyn's face, and she lifted the lantern with a hideous smile.

For one second the lantern seemed to hang there suspended, poised beside Nora's head.

"Welcome to Glanton House," she whispered.

Carolyn saw the blur as Joss hurtled forward. The impact knocked her sideways, and as she struggled for balance, Andy jerked her to her feet, frantically pulling at the gag and the ropes around her wrists. The lantern crashed to the wet floor beside the widow's walk, and with a yell, Andy flung himself toward it, knocking it outside, beating at the flames with his arms. Desperately Carolyn wriggled out of her jacket and threw it at him, screaming.

In the flickering gloom, Joss and Nora were indistinct shadows, their cries harsh and muffled as they wrestled together on the floor. As a shaft of lightning split the darkness, Carolyn saw Joss suddenly fall to one side, and Nora struggled free.

She aimed her gun straight at Carolyn.

From some far-off place, someone yelled Carolyn's name. As she realized she was about to die, Andy dived in front of her, and the gun went off.

The sound lasted forever.

It echoed on and on, like the thunder and lightning, the wind and the rain, and Carolyn couldn't tell anymore which sound was which—

In slow motion she saw Joss tackle Nora.

In slow motion she saw Andy fall.

She saw the blood all over him and the agony on his face . . .

And then she heard Nora shriek.

As Carolyn looked on in horror, Nora writhed upon the attic floor, her eyes huge and wild, her mouth gaping.

The gun was still clutched in her hand.

But as Joss stepped slowly away from her, Nora struggled to her knees, and Carolyn saw the hook protruding from her back.

In horrible fascination they watched Nora.

Watched as her face contorted in rage . . . as she staggered to her feet again . . . as she lifted the gun with shaking hands and once more aimed it at Carolyn.

Joss shoved her violently.

Nora gave a strangled cry, and as the gun flew out of her hand, she reeled back through the open doorway. For one split second her hands flailed uselessly at the air, clawing for one more breath of life.

Then her body pitched off the widow's walk into the raging darkness below.

27

"THE HOUSE LOOKS GREAT!" MRS. BAXTER SMILED FROM the front doorway. "Did you do all this yourself?"

"Well, with a little help from Jean. She's been finding books for me on how a sea captain's house might have looked a century or so ago."

Carolyn pushed her mother's wheelchair into the room and positioned it comfortably beside the fireplace.

"I really mean it!" Mrs. Baxter bounced excitedly in her chair, then gritted her teeth and laughed. "Ouch! Remind me not to get so happy, okay? It's too painful."

"There's still lots to do," Carolyn said, surveying the room with a sigh. "If you're still set on having guests."

"Well, of course I am! Do you think I'm going to let a little broken leg slow me down? I mean, when you think about it, this place has had *very minimal* problems."

"Minimal problems," Carolyn murmured with a wan smile. "Well . . . I guess that depends on your point of view."

"Oh, dear." Mom bit her lip and gestured Carolyn to come closer. "Honey, I don't mean to make light of all the hard work you've done. I know it's been rough, what with Joss leaving without a word and Nora dying like that—"

She broke off at the distressed look on Carolyn's face.

"Did they ever find out what happened to poor Nora?" she asked sympathetically, then shook her head in disbelief. "Imagine, finding her washed up like that on the beach . . ."

The thunder and the lightning and Nora's body disappearing over the broken railing—

"She must have fallen from the cliffs," Mrs. Baxter went on anxiously. "Or jumped, even. From what I've heard, no one's that surprised because she was so odd. But what a horrible way to die—all battered up like that—and after her warning *you* to stay away from the cliffs like she did—"

And Andy's arm was bleeding so bad, but somehow he and Joss finished untying me and got me downstairs to my room, but they made me promise to sit there and not look out any windows, they made me promise to sit there for a long, long time, and when I finally went out in the hall, hours and hours later, the attic door was closed, but it wasn't locked. . . .

"I guess we'll have to find someone else to help us," Mrs. Baxter concluded. "Hmmm . . . what about that nice boy who brought the groceries that morning? Do you remember him?"

And I went up there, but the attic was just an attic . . . an empty room with four walls, and no sign of a secret passageway. Lots of dust and cobwebs, and a wet floor where rain had leaked in, and a door that led out to a broken widow's walk. . . .

"I don't know what happened to him," Carolyn said, trying to focus in on her mother's questions. "I think he moved or something."

"That's too bad." Mom sighed. "He seemed like such a nice boy. And so did that Joss . . . but I guess you can't expect a drifter like him to want to stick around for any length of time."

"No," Carolyn murmured. "I guess you can't."

And after Nora's body finally washed up, the sheriff came by to ask some routine questions about her, and I told him that when she'd left here that evening, everything had been fine . . . just fine. . . .

"I wonder what will happen to him." Mrs. Baxter mused. "I wonder what he'll do with his life. I wonder if he'll ever care about anyone."

He told me he had to leave, and Andy looked so pale and weak standing there beside him, but he gave me a hug and said I'd be okay, that I'd always been okay— and I looked into Joss's eyes and he put his hand on my forehead to smooth back my hair. . . .

"I wonder if we'll ever even know?" Mrs. Baxter persisted.

And Joss said one more time . . . "You know I have to leave, Carolyn . . ." and he was smiling, "but this house has a way of bringing people back again," he said—and "Come on," Andy told him, "we've got to get out of here—"

And then Joss kissed me.

"Carolyn, are you all right?" Mom asked.

Carolyn shrugged. Suddenly she felt so sad.

"Still," Mom went on brightly, "you never know. Someday he just might be back this way again, and he might just decide to stop in and see us and see how the guest house is doing. Wouldn't that be wonderful?"

"Yes." Carolyn nodded, forcing a smile. "That would be wonderful."

"Hello!" a voice called behind them. "Anyone home?"

Carolyn turned and immediately smiled. "Jean, come on in—join the homecoming! Mom, this is my friend Jean I've been telling you about."

"I'm so glad to meet you!" Mrs. Baxter pumped Jean's hand warmly. "Carolyn's been telling me all about the research you've been helping her with. She's really getting this place into shape."

Jean hugged her and laughed. "Well, it might as well be authentic—and if I can suggest any historical decorating tips, I'm glad to do it. Oh, Carolyn, here's your mail. I stopped at the post office and thought I'd save you a trip."

"Thanks." Carolyn nodded. "I'll go make us some tea."

Leaving Jean and her mother to chat, Carolyn went to the kitchen. She flipped quickly through the stack of bills and letters and started to put them down on the table when one particular envelope caught her eye.

It was addressed to her.

The postmark was from Canada.

With trembling fingers Carolyn tore it open, her eyes hastily scanning the message written inside:

My dear Carolyn,

The night is stormy as I write this . . . it fills my head and heart with bittersweet memories. I don't know when this letter will reach you, or where I might be when it does . . . on some foreign sea, no doubt, exploring new and uncharted territories.

The journey has not been without its problems —or its dangers—but among my men there has been not one fatality, I'm happy to report.

Who can say what the future will bring? Perhaps someday we shall be reunited once more with those whose paths have crossed with ours.

The enclosed trinket is for you. I acquired it from a rather solitary gentleman who had no further use of it, and I knew at once that you should be the one to have it. Of itself it is worth very little . . . and yet the gentleman assured me it would bring you good fortune. When you wear it—and use it—I hope you will think of me.

Your loving Matthew

Carolyn stared down at the envelope. She tilted it up and let the contents slide out into her palm.

A necklace.

A tiny key on a delicate silver chain.

They never found Molly's body. And the next time I went down to the cave, it was as if no one had ever lived there at all. . . .

Yet somehow Carolyn knew that when she went to the beach this afternoon and made her way to the back of Molly's cave, that all she'd have to do was unlock the hidden door, and there it would be.

The golden hook.

Covered with jewels and sand and mystery, but not a trace of blood. . . .

"How's that tea coming?" Mom asked as Jean wheeled her into the kitchen.

"Just fine." Carolyn shoved the letter and chain into her pocket. "Ready in a second."

"Oh, honey, it's so good to be home." Mom patted Carolyn's hand and rested it against her cheek. "You *do* think it could be home now, don't you?"

Carolyn looked down at her mother's hopeful face. She lifted her eyes to the window, to the cold rainy morning, and then her heart quickened in her chest.

Was that something out there? Far off in the distance? Someone standing in the fog? Watching the house?

"Carolyn . . ." Her mother nudged her. "Do you think it *could* be?"

"I'm sure it could," Carolyn murmured, and she moved to the windowpane and gazed out at the endless gray world beyond. "And every single traveler will want to come here and stay."

She turned to her mother with a smile.

"Every one of them."

About the Author

Richie Tankersley Cusick loves to read and write scary books. Richie enjoys writing when it is rainy and gloomy outside, and likes to have a spooky soundtrack playing in the background. She writes at a desk that originally belonged to a funeral director in the 1800s and that she believes is haunted. Halloween is one of her favorite holidays. She and her husband decorate the entire house, which includes having a body laid out in state in the parlor, life-size models of Franken-stein's monster, the figure of Death to keep watch, and scary costumes for Hannah and Meg, their dogs. A neighbor recently told them that a previous owner of the house was feared by all of the neighborhood kids and no one would go to the house on Halloween.

Richie is the author of *Vampire, Fatal Secrets, The Locker, The Mall, Silent Stalker, Help Wanted, The Drifter,* and the novelization of *Buffy, the Vampire Slayer,* in addition to several adult novels for Pocket Books. She and her husband, Rick, live outside Kan-sas City, where she is currently at work on her next young adult novel.